ON THE BRINK

BERLIN FRACTURED SERIES, BOOK 2

MARION KUMMEROW

ON THE BRINKS, Berlin Fractured Series, Book 2

Marion Kummerow

CONTENTS

READER GROUP

Marion's Reader Group

Sign up for my reader group to receive exclusive background information and be the first one to know when a new book is released.

http://kummerow.info/subscribe

1

BRUNI

Berlin, January 1948

The singer and entertainer Brunhilde von Sinnen stepped out of the bathroom, a towel wrapped around her body and another like a turban around her hair. She glanced at the handsome man reclining on the mattress. He looked young for his forty-something years, although his cropped dark hair and mustache were graying. But his brown eyes were vivid, his mind sharp and his body well-toned.

It wasn't that she loved him, because love was an antiquated concept meant to enslave women and keep them in subservience to one man. But she was dearly attached to him for the way of life he provided her. In a Berlin still in shambles after World War Two, everything was scarce: food, accommodation, clothes, electricity.

1

Brigadier General Dean Harris was the Kommandant of the American sector and thus the most powerful man in Berlin – maybe with the exception of the Russian Kommandant General Sokolov.

She shivered at the thought of Sokolov, who was not only powerful but also one of the most unpleasant men she'd ever met. Pitch-black hair, a stocky appearance and a perpetually red nose, together with his irascible temper, fueled further by his ulcers, made him feared by friend and foe. She had no wish to share his bed.

No, Dean had been a stupendous catch and for more than a year now she'd lived a very comfortable life as his mistress. It was good business for both of them: she catered to all his needs for comfort and relaxation, while he provided luxuries for her that not many Germans could indulge in.

"How long can you stay?" she asked with a husky voice, setting the towel down on the dressing table and reaching for the silk robe Dean had given her several months earlier. It was a light pink color and softly hugged her naked skin.

"About that..." he answered evasively, rising from the bed, uncaring that he was stark naked as he strode for the bathroom door.

Alarmed, Bruni met him in the center of the room and ran a hand down his chest. But as she took a step closer, intending to plaster herself against him and lure him back to bed, he placed his hands on her shoulders and held her off.

She pouted up at him, her carefully made-up face having weathered their love-making very well – since she'd taken steps to touch it up, and her hair, in the bathroom a few moments ago.

Most people, even her dearest friends, considered her vain, but what was a girl to do? Her good looks were her capital. They had not only snagged Dean, but had also helped to bag the job as leading singer at the famous Café de Paris in the French sector, the hottest cabaret in town.

After all, no one wanted to watch an ugly woman sing. No, the mostly sex-starved soldiers craved a woman with curves and beauty to fuel their desires as they listened to her sultry voice move over them. And that was exactly what Bruni excelled at.

"What's wrong, lover?" She cocked her head to the side, studying the serious look on Dean's face.

He looked at her for a long moment and then stepped out of her reach. Instead of continuing on to the bathroom, he walked around the bed and pulled on his briefs and then his uniform pants. When he reached for his undershirt, Bruni realized he had no intention of sticking around for a repeat performance.

"You're leaving already?"

"Yes. My family arrives in Berlin this afternoon."

"Your wife? And your sons? What are they doing here?" Bruni suddenly felt dizzy. Of course, she'd known he was married, but his family was supposed to be far away in America.

"They have come to live here with me."

Bruni could tell that Dean found the current situation discomforting and as much as she longed to hurl insults at him for ditching her, she knew better. While their affair was nothing more than a business arrangement, they'd both grown fond of each other. Composing herself, she said in as matter-of-fact a voice as she could muster, "I assume this means we have to stop seeing each other."

"It does. You and I..." His voice faltered. "This is nothing personal, because I really liked you, but I'd rather we don't interact socially either. I love my wife."

I'm sure you do. Bruni pouted, but having used men for her benefit for so many years she knew it was over. And she also knew it was best for her not to have the most powerful man in Berlin for an enemy. "As you wish. I will forget that there ever was anything between us."

"I wouldn't have expected otherwise." He looked pleased. With a glance around the small apartment he said, "Naturally you can stay here and keep everything."

Rage snaked up her spine. How dare he even insinuate that he'd evict her from this place and make her live in one of the despicable holes most everyone else had to put up with? She was Brunhilde von Sinnen, not some random German Fräulein he could toss away. But she kept her voice low and sultry when she answered him, "It was nice while it lasted. I wish you happy times with your family."

Then she turned on her heel and disappeared into the bathroom, confident he'd let himself out before she returned.

That selfish fool just dumped me! Men can't be trusted!

She carefully arranged her platinum blonde curls, placed deliberately in a style very similar to the one Ginger Rogers was fond of. Putting the final touches on her appearance, Bruni allowed herself to wallow in self-pity.

This breakup was so much worse than what her Soviet lover Feodor Orlovski had pulled off. After the failed elections in October 1946 he'd simply disappeared, never to be seen or heard of again.

When she heard the door close, she left the bathroom and changed the bedsheets. No need to be reminded of Dean by his scent. She sure as hell wouldn't pine for him with a broken heart, but she would dearly miss his money and the perks that came with sleeping with an American general.

"You bastard!" she shouted at the wall.

His brazenness in tossing her aside angered her to no end and she cursed, ranted and bitched about Dean, until she finally stopped. It would only cause wrinkles in her otherwise flawless visage. To heal her hurt pride, and to guarantee her lifestyle, she needed to bewitch another Allied officer, preferably an American. But that project would have to wait until late afternoon, when she began working in the Café de Paris.

Meanwhile she would pay her friend Marlene a visit. Maybe she would commiserate.

She caught Marlene during lunch break at university when she emerged from the building amongst a group of fellow law students.

"Hello, Marlene," she yelled.

Marlene, a tall and slender brunette with soft wavy hair and big blue eyes, broke out into a smile when she saw Bruni and came over to give her a big hug. "What a surprise, Bruni. What brings you here? Have you finally decided to enroll at university?"

"Me? Not on your life." Despite her bad mood Bruni had to laugh. Just the thought of sticking her nose into boring textbooks made her skin crawl. "Want to have lunch with me?"

Going out for lunch was a luxury Marlene normally couldn't afford, so she eagerly jumped at the opportunity. "Sure. Let's go."

Automatically Bruni steered toward a small place that catered mostly to American officers, before changing her mind and instead walking toward a much more modest place.

At the sight of the shabby restaurant Marlene gave her a critical look and then asked, "What's wrong?"

"I'll tell you inside." Once they'd ordered a meal from the menu reserved for those who paid in foreign currency, she said without further ado, "Dean dumped me."

"He what?"

"Yes, he dumped me. His family is here."

"Here? As in, here in Berlin?"

Bruni nodded. "They arrive this afternoon."

"Oh! That's quite surprising. But you knew this would eventually happen, right?"

"How can you be so indifferent? I'm heartbroken!"

"It's not like you loved him."

Bruni opened her mouth to argue and then realized it wasn't worth the effort. Marlene knew her too well. "Fine, I didn't love him."

Marlene smirked. "What you truly loved is the perks and presents Dean provided for you."

"I'm not saying I don't like nice things…" Bruni shook her blonde curls. She held the same opinion as Lorelei Lee in the novel *Gentlemen Prefer Blondes* and considered diamonds a girl's best friends.

"You're completely spoiled and Dean was willing to buy you things in order to have your company. It was an equal trade agreement…"

"Let me guess, you're studying business law this semester?" Bruni asked with barely concealed sarcasm in her voice.

"Don't pretend to be offended. You're just miffed because your pride got trampled on. You normally run the table and do the dumping. He just beat you to it."

Bruni huffed out a breath. So much for commiseration. Apparently, Marlene had decided to pour salt onto Bruni's wounds instead. "Hear my words: Dean's going to regret bringing his family here."

Marlene laughed at her unspoken threat. "What do you imagine might happen? Sokolov challenging him to a duel for the hurt he's inflicted on you?"

Bruni's efforts to keep a serene expression soon collapsed and she broke out into a giggle. "That would be nice, wouldn't it? Not that I fancy Sokolov."

"Ugghh…who would? Apart from looking the part of the beast, his abusive rants and spiteful propaganda are hard to stomach. I wonder whether he himself believes that bunch of lies he bestows upon us every single day."

For a while they ate in silence. The meal certainly wasn't up to the standard Bruni was used to, but Marlene didn't seem to mind.

"That was delicious. Thanks for inviting me," Marlene said after she cleared her plate.

Only then did it dawn on Bruni that she'd have to find a new benefactor fast if she didn't want to tighten her belt and join the misery of the rest of Berlin's population. It was a scary prospect.

She needed to find another Allied soldier, an officer – nothing less would do – enlisted men didn't have the salary and connections to grant her the lifestyle she craved.

"Still feeling sorry for yourself?" Marlene interrupted her thoughts.

"No." Bruni grinned. "Plotting my next moves."

"Who's the lucky guy?"

"I haven't decided yet, since there are some requirements he needs to fulfill." She counted them on her fingers. "Allied man, preferably American. Officer, with at least the rank of a captain. Stationed in Berlin for more than a few weeks. Preferably without a wife back home. Not ugly as sin."

"Well, good luck with that."

"I don't need luck. I have my charms." She bestowed a gracious smile upon Marlene and blew her a kiss. "No one can resist these looks."

Marlene broke into a fit of giggles. "I'm sure they can't. I already pity the poor man who's going to be your next target. He won't even know what hit him."

2

_____

VICTOR

March 20, 1948

Sergeant Victor Richards stepped out of the train arriving at the shattered Berlin Zoo station. He'd been supposed to fly in, but Victor hated flying with a passion that was unexplainable, considering his job – an airport engineer.

He'd seen his share of ruins at the Rhein-Main airport in Frankfurt, where his task was the maintenance of the airport buildings. Although maintenance was the wrong word; it was actually more like reconstructing the whole damn thing from nothing but rubble. He'd always envied his friends who worked at the much neater, less damaged Wiesbaden airport, but the second he disembarked the military train in Berlin he vowed to never again complain about desolate conditions.

If Frankfurt was bad, there were no words to describe the utter misery he found in Berlin. He didn't have much time to ponder just how atrocious this city looked, because moments later, a jeep arrived and a young soldier jumped out. "Are you Sergeant Richards?"

"Yes."

"Hop in. I'll drive you to the Allied Control Council in Schöneberg."

"Thanks, man." He shouldered his kitbag and jumped into the open car. They drove in silence and Victor was left alone with his thoughts. General Clay had requested an expert on airport maintenance to participate in the upcoming four-power meeting, and Victor's clueless commanding officer had been all too happy to send him instead.

Normally he wasn't nervous when talking about his field of expertise, but he'd heard so many horrible stories about the Soviet abuse both in the Kommandatura, the governing body of Berlin, and the Allied Control Council that governed all of Germany.

Would Marshal Kapralov, the Head of the Soviet Military Administration in Germany, shower him with insults the same way he had so many others before him? And what would General Clay say if Victor couldn't answer some of the Soviet's questions satisfactorily? He felt a slight unease creeping up his stomach – a simple sergeant like him going up against a marshal?

"Here we are," his driver said, tearing Victor out of his musings.

He'd never before been at the Allied Control Council and

was quite surprised at how beautiful it looked. The majestic stone building, formerly hosting the Kammergericht, the superior Court of Justice, showed little war damage. The neo-baroque façade displayed five floors with a prominent central projection, which the Germans called *Risalit*, adorned by columns, pilaster and figurines. The flags of the four occupying powers flew over the large front doors.

"Quite impressive, eh?" the driver said and then continued with an explanation about the building. "It has a total of five hundred rooms, thirty-eight aisles and seven courtyards. But we use only the middle part for the ACC and the northern aisle for the Berlin Air Safety Center."

"Yes, thank you," Victor answered and jumped out of the jeep. After the usual security checks, he was led into the meeting room, where several other members had already taken their seats.

He settled down with the American delegation, took out his documents and meticulously arranged them on the desk in front of him. Whatever question the council wanted to throw at him, he was prepared.

As usual he'd prepared answers to everything even remotely connected to the topic, even though he knew the bosses would probably want to know less than ten percent of it. But it was never a bad thing to be overprepared. This same trait had saved many lives during the advance through France.

The tension in the room was thick enough to cut with a knife; Victor wondered what had happened in the morning. He didn't have to wait long for an answer.

Marshal Kapralov opened the afternoon session

demanding full transparency about the secret resolutions made at the illegal London conference.

Victor's head began aching. Secret resolutions? The decisions had been made public to everyone. Illegal London conference? The Soviets had declined the invitation. Was he missing something?

Nervously he leafed through the papers on his desk. There was nothing in there about any illegal meetings or secret decisions.

Kapralov then directly addressed General Clay, demanding that he reverse any and all decisions taken in London, because all questions pertaining to Germany were under the responsibility of the Allied Control Council.

General Clay politely refused Kapralov's demand and Victor could see how the Soviet Marshal's face turned purple, before he spewed out an avalanche of insults. Despite not speaking a single word of Russian beyond *nyet* and *nastrovje*, Victor didn't have to wait for the translation to understand the meaning.

But when the translator talked, his eyes almost popped out.

"This is the most serious violation of Allied obligations as written down in the Potsdam Agreement and subsequent Four-Power Agreements. If the USA, Great Britain and France are not willing to be held accountable to written contracts, they are nothing better than common criminals in the streets of Berlin. The hideous London resolutions are an attack on peace and democracy in Germany."

Victor panted. He looked left and right, before his eyes honed in on General Clay, who didn't flinch. Victor couldn't believe that Clay stayed silent at such an outrageous insult from the Russian. But the general didn't utter a word, did not even roll an eye. It was the most peculiar situation Victor had experienced in his life.

The translator continued, "You have created a situation where the Soviet side is held solely accountable, whereas the Western allies refuse to do the same. With these shameful actions you are proving that you don't respect the Four-Power governance over Germany and have turned the Allied Control Council into a farce."

This couldn't be true, or could it? Victor was so baffled, he leaned over to the man sitting to his right and asked, "Is he really saying this?"

The other man, Colonel Wilder, seemed to be quite used to these kinds of shenanigans and whispered, "I gather this is your first time in our circus. But don't worry, when Kapralov is done accusing us of every crime under the sun, he'll calm down and come up with some ridiculous demand that we can't accept, just to prove his point. Several hours later Kapralov, in his role as current chairman, will close the meeting without any results."

Victor looked with dismay at the bunch of papers in front of him and the hours of work he'd put into preparing them. It was devastating to know that he might not even have to present his case.

The next moment Marshal Kapralov took the floor again and a murmur went through the room from those who understood Russian. Victor watched stupefied when Kapralov left the room, even while the translator still spoke. The sixteen-man Soviet delegation also rose as a unit and followed their leader from the room.

"The Allied Control Council no longer exists as an organ of government," the translator said.

The door closed.

The Generals Clay, Robertson and König looked mildly surprised, but not overly shocked. Victor was shattered. Had he just witnessed the end of Four-Power rule over Germany?

"A deliberate discourtesy," Clay commented dryly.

"Well, that's that," the man to Victor's left commented softly.

Another one said, "We've seen this coming for some time. Good riddance, I'd say."

For a while it seemed unclear what to do, because according to process the chairman – Kapralov – had to officially close the meeting.

"I guess the meeting is closed," General Clay said, and made to leave the room. Everyone followed him. The atmosphere was quite peculiar. Victor sensed tension, disbelief, and relief all at the same time. He grabbed his papers and followed the American delegation outside.

Suddenly with a lot of free time on his hands, he took the offered transport to the garrison and asked some of the younger men, "Hey, where's the place to have some fun tonight?"

"You new here? I'm John, by the way."

"Just for a few days, my home base is Rhein-Main airport."

"Well then, welcome to the capital!" John grinned. "If you want, I'll take you to the Café de Paris tonight. Best place in town, and the star singer? A blonde bombshell. Easily compares to Marlene Dietrich." John licked his lips with a dreamy expression.

"Sounds good," Victor said, although he wasn't especially keen on blondes. In his experience there were few authentic ones, and the rest he considered shallow.

3

BRUNI

"Hey, doll. You're up next," Gabi called out as she walked into the dressing room behind the stage.

Bruni looked up from the small dressing table where she was applying her stage makeup. "Good crowd tonight."

"Sure is. Plenty of handsome soldiers. One of them looks like Cary Grant when he was young and yummy." Gabi waggled her eyebrows and the other girls in the room chuckled.

Bruni rolled her eyes and then said, "You're engaged, or did you forget?"

"No, but I can still look. Right?"

"As long as that soldier boy of yours doesn't see," another of the women called from the back.

Bruni nodded. "Don't bite the hand that feeds you. If Sam sees you making eyes at another man, he won't be pleased."

"So, are you going to get friendly with anyone tonight?" Gabi asked, sitting down on a chair next to Bruni's.

"Maybe. With Dean gone I need someone new, but I'm picky."

"No, you're spoiled."

Bruni wrinkled her nose. "Second time one of my friends has said that about me today – do you think there's some truth to it?"

Peals of laughter filled the room and Bruni gazed from one girl to the next. "And you know what? You bet your ass I am. What's the point in fawning over a man unless he's willing to keep me in the style I deserve?"

Gabi shook her head and headed for her own dressing table. "I'll leave young Cary Grant to you."

"Thank you, I appreciate it, but you don't have to do me any favors." Bruni took one last look at her reflection, admiring her perfect platinum curls and the artfully done makeup enhancing her blue eyes. She pursed her painted ruby red lips for a moment, hoping she might find someone worthy of her attentions in the audience tonight. She was tired of being alone and quickly running out of money, since Dean's generous provisions had stopped coming.

"Bruni, you're up."

"Gotta go wow the boys," she told the others as she headed for the stage curtain. She stepped into the wing and glanced out, surveying the place and trying to identify the new faces Gabi had mentioned. The lights only afforded her a view of the tables nearest to the stage, and beyond that all she could see was blackness.

The stage manager nodded at her and she picked up the microphone and stepped out to raucous applause. Giving a flirtatious smile to the men clapping enthusiastically for her, she walked to the center of the stage. The pianist played the first strains of her song and excitement overcame her. Moments later she filled the cabaret with her husky voice, low and sultry, singing about lost love and the end of loneliness, while she expertly flirted with her body and her facial expressions.

She finally caught a glimpse of the man Gabi had been raving about, and Bruni had to admit her colleague possessed excellent taste. The man was gorgeous. More than gorgeous.

He was wearing an American uniform, but from this distance Bruni couldn't make out his rank. She flirted with him, drawing his attention on the off chance that he was looking for a bit of company later. Tall, with broad shoulders, and pronounced muscles, his dirty-blond hair tousled despite its shortness, he was just the way she liked her men. Although looks came last on her list of requirements.

She noticed that he was watching her like a hawk and she preened as she finished her song, making sure he knew that she was singing exclusively for him. Sally, one of the waitresses, stopped beside his table and just as Bruni hoped, he said something to the waitress while gesturing toward the stage.

Not for nothing was Bruni considered a master of this game. She'd had to learn at a very young age to use her looks for survival. Had wrapped men around her little finger, offering her favors in exchange for food, shelter and fondness, although never for love. Love was but an illusion, something better to stay far away from.

When Sally approached the side of the stage, Bruni hid her satisfied expression and feigned surprise.

"The gentleman at table number six would like you to join him for a drink."

Bruni glanced at him, pleased to see that he was still watching her. She appeared to think about his request for a moment and then nodded. "Tell him I'll join him in a few minutes."

Sally returned with her message and Bruni smiled coyly at him, before slipping behind the stage curtain. She entered the dressing room to the hoots and hollers from her fellow performers.

"That boy was eating out of your hand," Gabi said with honest admiration.

Bruni beamed and touched up her lipstick. "He invited me to have a drink with him."

"I don't know why I ever worried about you."

"It's just for a drink. I'm not even sure what his rank is."

"And of course, that would matter to you." Gabi shook her head as she slipped her arms into her coat. "Sam's a sergeant, but he takes good care of me."

"Let's just hope this one doesn't have a wife and kids waiting to fly over here and join him." Bruni fluffed up her hair one last time, before she headed out into the bar area and approached Mr. Gorgeous on quiet feet. From close up he was even more attractive, and her pulse ratcheted up. He sensed her coming and rose to pull out a vacant chair for her. Bruni cast him her most charming smile and then had to force the smile to stay in place when she saw his rank stripes. Disappointment seeped deep into her bones. Why did the truly gorgeous ones always have to be on the low end of the pecking order?

"Thank you for joining me," he said in a deep and gravelly voice that sent irrational tingles down her limbs. Bruni glanced at the chair and then back up into his grey-green eyes.

"Am I so ugly that you changed your mind?" he asked with a small upturn of his lip.

"No, not at all…" Her knees wobbled and she wanted to feel his arms wrapped around her. She reminded herself that this wasn't about superfluous emotions, but about business. She needed a new benefactor and couldn't waste her charms on random men. If he wasn't at least a captain, he wasn't suitable, because on a lower rank's salary, he would never be able to afford the luxuries she needed. What was worse, if she went out with him, she would appear to be easy, and then she'd soon be flooded with inappropriate offers from inappropriate men.

"My name is Victor Richards," he said, and his wonderful eyes kept staring into hers. It was like he was exercising some kind of spell over her.

"Brunhilde von Sinnen, but my friends call me Bruni," she replied automatically.

"Well, Bruni. Would you like to keep me company for a few minutes? Your performance on stage was phenomenal. It moved me."

"It did?" It was a stupid thing to say, but for whatever reason, her brains had turned to mush and she couldn't think of a single clever-witted line. He was pointing at the chair he was holding out for her and she slowly lowered herself down to sit on the edge.

Being so near to him took her breath away – and her ability to think clearly, which was never a good thing. She should get up and walk away. Now! But her legs refused to obey and even her traitorous face broke into a stupid smile.

He returned her smile and she couldn't help but admire his physique. As he sat down, Sally returned. "What can I get you to drink?"

Victor looked at her with a raised brow and Bruni felt her insides tremble. *God, he's beyond gorgeous.*

"I'll take a martini." She saw the slight smirk on Sally's face and knew that the waitress would watch her with a hawk's eyes and hurry to tell everyone in the kitchen the gossip about Bruni and Victor.

Victor ordered another beer, and as soon as the waitress disappeared toward the bar, he leaned over, smiling. Bruni noticed the deep-cut dimples, and her resolve to stay away from him melted like ice in the sunshine. Having one drink with him wouldn't hurt. But then she'd be on her way.

"My pals told me you sing like Marlene Dietrich, but they were wrong. You're so much better."

Bruni flushed at the praise, which was absolutely extraordinary for her to do, and as he looked at her, her own eyes were drawn to the laugh lines at the corners of his eyes. This was a man who enjoyed life, and she shouldn't find it as appealing as she did.

She glanced around the cabaret, half-hoping someone would come up and rescue her. But the regulars knew that while she generously flirted with all of them, she never went out with a customer, unlike most of the other girls.

So why did she accept a drink from this stranger? The only thing he had going for him was his gorgeousness. Dirty blond hair that was pushed back from his forehead, a strong chin, and eyes that a girl could get lost in. He was tanned, making her think that he spent a considerable amount of time outdoors.

There was a hint of a beard growing along his jawline, and she itched to touch the stubble. He apparently was one of those men who needed to shave twice if he wanted to maintain a smooth face. Why that turned her on, she couldn't say, but she suddenly had an image of him standing before a mirror, his hips wrapped in a towel and his chest bare, as he applied a razor to his skin.

Stop it, Bruni! This man isn't for you.

Thankfully the waitress returned to interrupt her silly pining. Bruni gratefully accepted the drink and toasted to Victor before she sipped it, eyeing him over the rim of her glass.

"Have you always lived in Berlin?" Victor asked, trying to draw her into conversation.

"Yes."

"I was shocked at how much damage was done to the city."

Bruni nodded. "Despite the way it looks these days, I still love my city and would never want to live anywhere else." She truly, honestly loved Berlin; in contrast to a man, her beloved city would never betray her, dump her or hurt her. "How long have you been here?"

"Just arrived this morning. I'll be here for two days and then I must return to Frankfurt am Main."

"You are stationed in Frankfurt?" Another reason not to waste time on him.

"Yes, at the Rhein-Main airport, although..." his eyes twinkled with mischief, "...we usually call it Rhein-Mud."

Bruni couldn't help but giggle. "Not a very nice sobriquet."

"And not a very nice place to work. I swear, since I arrived there half a year ago, it's been raining every single day and we're walking knee deep in mud." He made a squishing sound and she laughed again.

"I'm sure you must be exaggerating."

"You don't believe me?" He made a hurt puppy face and put a hand to his chest. "I'm floored."

This man was hilarious. "Seriously, knee deep?" Bruni had difficulties keeping a straight face.

"If I say so myself. And it's a wonder that our planes can even take off, stuck like flotsam in quicksand."

"Now I know you're exaggerating."

"Maybe a teeny-weeny bit." Victor raised a hand and put forefinger and thumb about half an inch apart to show her how little, while his twinkling eyes did funny things to her insides. Since he'd leave Berlin for good in two days' time, what harm would it do to spend the night with him? He wasn't going to expect anything from her, and nobody would have to know.

Once he left for Frankfurt she'd continue her quest to find a new benefactor, but meanwhile she'd enjoy his company. It was a rare occasion that she laughed with so much abandon in the drab environment that Berlin presented.

Having taken that decision, she stopped caring about her long list of qualities a man needed to have and enjoyed the fun of being with Victor.

"Did you already get to see something of Berlin?" she asked.

"Not really, I arrived this morning and headed straight to Schöneberg."

"The Allied Control Council?" Bruni asked, her appreciation for him soaring.

"Yes, but I'm only a lowly expert for airport construction and security." He looked at her for a few long moments, apparently unsure what to say next. "You probably heard it already on the radio..."

She shook her head. "I never listen to the radio before going on stage, it distracts me."

"Do you want me to distract you now?" His gravelly voice made her heart jump.

"What?"

"With the news you'll otherwise hear in the morning."

Her eyes riveted to his full and kissable lips, she nodded.

"The Allied Control Council is no more. Marshal Kapralov and his stooges walked out today."

Bruni cocked her head, not fully understanding the implications, but when the momentousness of what Victor had just said hit her, she gasped. "You're not joking, are you?"

"Unfortunately not."

She composed herself. "That was to be expected. I'm actually surprised it lasted this long." Dean had often told her about General Sokolov's attacks in the Kommandatura and she assumed that Sokolov's superior Kapralov would put on a similar show in the ACC. Naturally she wouldn't tell Victor that. One of the things the men liked in Bruni was that she never revealed the information they confided to her in private.

He laughed out loud and again the cutest dimples

appeared on his cheeks. "The good thing is, now I have nothing to do for the next two days until I'm scheduled to return to Frankfurt."

"Would you like me to show you Berlin? Tomorrow's my day off." Bruni could barely believe she had actually offered this.

"They give you an entire day off? And what about the night?" Victor asked with mischief in his eyes.

She cast him a playfully reprimanding look. "Don't get any ideas, soldier. I'm doing this out of the goodness of my heart to show a foreign guest the beauties of my city. Although…your colleagues didn't leave a stone unturned during the war."

He made a slightly guilty face and she hurried to lighten up the atmosphere by saying, "We do have a flattering sobriquet too. Berlin is called the world's biggest heap of rubble."

He raised his beer and said, "To the rubble, and to the world's most amazing woman."

"So, it's a deal then?"

"A deal?" He scratched his stubble. "So far you have offered to show me around. Where's the catch? What's expected of me in return?"

"No catch at all. You simple need to keep me in good humor while I'm your tourist guide."

"That I can do." He showed her a row of perfect white teeth.

"And that includes keeping me well fed."

"I see. Do I have to cook myself or can I take you out to a restaurant?"

Bruni wrinkled her forehead as if thinking hard and

then slowly said, "A restaurant would do, I think...if it's a French one."

"Fine with me. I'd rather not go into the Soviet sector after what happened today, but let me guess, the restaurant you have in mind is in the French sector?"

"How did you know?" she asked him coyly, batting her eyelashes.

Victor shrugged and grinned. His dimples appeared and made him look even more adorable. "Just a lucky guess. When do I pick you up?"

Bruni gave him the time and the address.

"I'll be there. I'm looking forward to seeing you again," he said, touching the back of her hand briefly where it lay on the table between them. "As for right now, I should get back to the barracks and get some sleep. It's been a very long day. Can I escort you home?"

Bruni shook her head and lifted up her partially finished drink. She had a reputation to keep and didn't want anyone to notice her interest in this man. "I have to go on stage one more time. I'll see you tomorrow."

"You bet you will." Victor stood up and put on his cap. "I'm glad I came here tonight. Meeting you has definitely brightened up my day."

"Glad I could help." She gave him a flirtatious smile to go with her words. "I'm lucky I caught your eye tonight."

"You would catch a blind man's eye. You, Fräulein von Sinnen, are stunning, and I know I'll be the envy of every man in the restaurant tomorrow night." Victor lifted up her hand and then placed a kiss on the palm, his eyes never leaving hers.

She felt his kiss all the way to her toes and her core

clenched when he folded her fingers over the place where his warm lips had contacted her skin. "Until tomorrow."

Bruni's voice refused to work, and she nodded, watching him stride away a moment later. She lowered her hand to her lap, keeping her fingers closed for several long seconds as she savored the conversation with him.

4

VLADI

Vladimir Rublev yawned and glanced at his alarm clock. It was already past noon, but after the beastly party last night he wasn't in a hurry to get out of bed. Nobody in the Soviet administration would be at work this early anyway.

About ten minutes later he got up, walked to the sink in the corner of the room and held his head under the faucet. The cold water cleared his foggy, hung-over brains and he grinned. After Marshal Kapralov's coup the day before, spontaneous celebrations had started and vodka had flowed until early in the morning.

Should the Western Allies stick the quadripartite ruling up their asses, it served them right after harassing their Soviet counterparts for the better part of three years. Their entire presence in Berlin was a ploy to attack Russia and force their damaging capitalist theories onto the Soviet people.

He towel-dried his cropped blond hair and put on his

uniform. As a member of Red Army Intelligence, he wasn't required to wear a uniform and normally he preferred a pair of sturdy pants, a shirt with the top two buttons left open and a leather jacket, just like his idol the heavyweight boxing champion of the USSR, Nikolay Korolyov.

Vladimir, or Vladi as his friends called him, had done some boxing during his adolescent years, but had soon found it more lucrative to follow in his father's footsteps and become a member of the GUR, Red Army Intelligence.

But today, he felt like wearing the uniform. After such a historic humiliation of the imperialist enemy, it would add just a touch of gravitas to his appearance.

When he arrived at Soviet Military Administration Headquarters in Karlshorst, he was surprised to find General Sokolov, the Soviet Kommandant of Berlin, already in his office.

"Good morning, Comrade General," Vladi greeted him. "It was quite the temper tantrum the Americans threw yesterday, making Comrade Kapralov have to walk out on them."

"Good morning, Comrade Rublev, good that you're here. I urgently need a man who isn't afraid to stir up a hornet's nest."

Vladi silently cursed. "Naturally, Comrade General. What can I do?"

"Board a train."

It was quite unusual for Sokolov to be in a joking mood, and Vladi dutifully chuckled while cursing himself for getting up so early. He should have slept an hour longer and the general might have found someone else to carry out whatever idea he'd cooked up.

General Sokolov beckoned him to sit down. "Now that the Americans have finally shown their true colors and refused to do their duty according to the Four-Power governance, we need to show them that we're not weaklings to be shoved around."

Vladi nodded and made a mental note on the new line of argument that the Americans had refused to work in the ACC, not that Kapralov had walked out.

"I want you to gather a team of military police and stop all Allied trains through our zone with the demand to inspect freight and passengers due to a severe smuggling problem."

Vladi gasped. "You mean the Western military trains in transit from Berlin to their zones in Germany, Comrade General?" That was a clear violation if not of written agreements, then of customary law. As long as the other Allies didn't deviate from the stipulated highways and train routes on their transit through the Soviet-occupied zone, the Soviets had no right to check up on military personnel or goods.

"Exactly. Tell them we need to take desperate measures against contraband. The Western Allies are dismantling Berlin industry and shipping the equipment to their zones in Western Germany. This is a clear violation of the Potsdam Agreement, which we won't accept. Those Americans truly have no shame."

"Yes, Comrade General, I'll immediately get to work and start controlling trains tomorrow morning."

"Keep me posted, and..." Sokolov stared at Vladi. "...keep to rabble-rousing, but don't give them a reason to retaliate.

Avoid a major conflict at all costs. We don't want to go to war over this, at least not yet."

"Understood." Vladi turned on his heel and left the office. Maybe his newly assigned task wasn't half bad. He'd have some fun harassing the Americans and might even be lucky enough to spend the night at the border in Helmstedt, where he had a willing girl waiting for him.

When the alarm rang at seven a.m. the next morning, Vladi revised his opinion about the new task. Why on earth did he have to get up in the middle of the night, while everyone else could still slumber for another three to four hours?

He consoled himself with the fact that he'd soon be able to take out his foul mood on the imperialists, and got up to shave. Personally, he considered it more effectual to be unshaved when embarking on one of the shadier missions, but since he'd be in uniform and delivering needle pricks without stirring up too much trouble, he wanted to look respectable.

In front of the mirror he practiced a friendly, yet determined, expression, followed by the raise of an eyebrow when saying, "I'm very sorry for the inconvenience, but due to a recent surge in illegal contraband ..."

Finished with his rehearsal, he combed his hair with his fingers and then left in the American-provided Lend-Lease jeep – it had been rebranded with a Russian insignia – for the town of Brandenburg.

The train station of Brandenburg was about halfway from Berlin to the inner-German border and deep enough in the Soviet-occupied zone to make the passengers think twice whether they wanted to refuse a Soviet inspection and be sent back to Berlin, or happily travel on.

As far as he knew, no important American officers would travel on the morning train to Hannover, but one could never be too sure, because those stubborn louts refused to give complete passenger lists to the Soviets, claiming sovereign power over their military trains.

In Brandenburg he met up with five local military police and instructed them on the task at hand. He impressed on them not to pull their guns under any circumstances, because the Americans were known to shoot first and ask questions later. Then he waited for the train.

The stationmaster activated the switch and signaled the train to halt. It came to a standstill with loud puffing and Vladi smiled with giddy anticipation. *Let the fun begin!*

"Here we go." He indicated the railcar they were to board. As expected, it was full of uniformed men and just a few women and children, supposedly military families. Much to his relief there was no senior officer aboard that railcar. The officers had the annoying habit of making decisions without consulting headquarters, and might have foiled his mission.

With two of the military police in tow he entered a compartment with a woman and two children passengers, and one sleeping soldier in the corner and said in his best English, "Ma'am, can I see your papers please?"

She looked up at him, and her eyes went round when she recognized his uniform. *Well done. She's afraid and because of her children she won't put up a fuss.*

"My papers? We are American military – I thought there wouldn't be any Russian inspections for us?"

"I'm very sorry for the inconvenience, ma'am, but due to a recent surge in illegal contraband we have to scrutinize every person passing through our territory." He gave her a reassuring smile, hoping she'd see him as a helpful officer.

She looked slightly at unease, but opened her oversized handbag and rummaged for her papers.

Vladi was very pleased; so far everything was working according to plan. He'd look at her papers and then order her to open all three suitcases in the luggage rack, before he'd continue to the next compartment. He wondered how long it would take until someone got impatient and tried to find out the reason for their unplanned halt in Brandenburg. Then the real fun would begin.

She handed him the papers for her and the two children, while the man in the corner snored through the entire operation. *Just as well*, Vladi thought while giving the papers a cursory glance. Mrs. Harris and her two children. He almost toppled over. This was the wife of the American Kommandant in Berlin. If her husband was on the train as well, there'd be hell to pay.

He glanced at the soldier in the corner. Definitely an enlisted man, maybe some kind of bodyguard for the Kommandant's wife. Cold sweat running down Vladi's back, he racked his brain to consider his next moves. No, her husband couldn't be aboard, or he would travel in the same compartment with his family – and he thought hard to remember the date for the next meeting at the Kommandatura. He was pretty sure it was scheduled for the next day.

No, Brigadier General Dean Harris definitely couldn't be on board.

Emboldened by his analysis, he returned the papers to her and said, "Thank you so much, Mrs. Harris. And I'm terribly sorry, but would you allow me a look into your suitcase?"

"No," she said.

That, he hadn't expected. *Stupid cow, don't get cheeky with me.* He forced his expression to stay neutral, but frowned. "Unfortunately, according to the Quadripartite Rulings for Prevention of Contraband, all goods leaving the Soviet-occupied zone are subject to scrutiny at the Soviet Union's sole discretion."

She returned his stare for long seconds, before she succumbed. "Alright." Then she stood and pointed to the smallest of the suitcases in the rack: "You can start with this one."

Vladi suppressed a smirk and moved threateningly close to her while he heaved the suitcase down from the rack. It weighed a ton and he wondered what she was transporting in there. Gold bullion? In that case he'd confiscate it.

Just when he dropped the suitcase onto one of the empty seats, the younger one of the boys cried out, "Hey, that's mine. Get your hands off!"

And there went his carefully devised plan. The soldier in the corner woke up, assessed the situation with a single glance and jumped to his feet. "What are you doing in here?"

"I'm conducting a search in the name of the Soviet Union." Vladi read the name Johnson on the other man's nametag. He'd barely finished the sentence when Johnson said much too loudly, "You have no right to conduct any searches. This is a military train, property of the United States of America."

"I'm afraid this is not true. Your train is passing through our territory, so we have every right to search its passengers and goods – especially in the case of imminent danger."

The soldier positioned himself between Vladi and the woman and said, "And what kind of phony danger are we dealing with, exactly?"

"Contraband. Your papers, please, Johnson." Vladi stretched out his hand in a demanding gesture, his fingertips all but touching the chest of the American. He could sense the wrath bubbling up inside the other man and hoped the soldier would commit a stupid mistake that enabled Vladi to arrest him.

"No."

"Just show them to him, and he'll leave us alone," whispered Mrs. Harris.

Vladi nodded. "See, soldier, this woman is wise. I'm not here to cause trouble, I have my orders to protect the property of the great Soviet Union and the German people."

The soldier scoffed. "I'll alert the ranking officer in the train."

Vladi felt his muscles tense as he prepared to shove the other man back. But the short clearing of a throat behind him assured him that the local military policeman was blocking the compartment door and there was no way Johnson could actually leave without shoving him aside, which would inevitably lead to a kerfuffle and Johnson's arrest.

He saw the realization hit Johnson's eyes, followed by a barely conceivable sagging of his shoulder.

"Your papers, please?" Vladi said in his most polite voice, carefully keeping out any trace of triumph.

Johnson sent him a stare that could kill, but obeyed and handed over his papers.

"Corporal Johnson, your home base is Wiesbaden. What were you doing in Berlin?"

"None of your business," Johnson growled. Mrs. Harris winced and shielded her two sons, whom Vladi estimated to be eight and ten years old, with her own body. It felt good to see the fear in her eyes. She didn't have to know that he'd never physically harm a woman.

"It is completely my business, since I'm protecting the interests of my country and you could be a black marketeer." He decided to let the interrogation go, since this Johnson was beyond stubborn and might do something outright stupid. Something that might cause a diplomatic incident and lots of red tape.

Strong-arming and harassing was expected, but Sokolov would not be pleased to receive a frantic phone call from the hysterical Beast of Berlin, Dean Harris.

"I'm afraid I have to have a look into your bags," Vladi said.

"They're in the luggage rack," Johnson hissed.

So, he was about to play difficult, just what Vladi had looked forward to. He turned around and motioned for his colleague, who then pulled the duffle bag down, rather roughly, and poured the contents onto an empty seat. Vladi donned white gloves and rifled through the things, holding the underwear up for inspection.

Mrs. Harris, naturally, was a married woman with two sons of her own and didn't even raise an eyebrow, but the young corporal flushed purple to see his intimate wear exposed in front of a lady. Then Vladi found a package of condoms and smirked. "What's this?"

"You know damn well what this is," Johnson said, his face growing more purple with every passing second.

"I really don't know. What do you call them? Jimmy bags? Care to explain what you need this for?" Vladi planted his feet, keeping his arms and hands relaxed by his sides and resisting the urge to reach for the weapon at his hip. Those louts were known to shoot immediately when threatened.

Johnson was now clearly desperate, avoiding even a glance in the direction of Mrs. Harris and her underage sons. "There's a lady present."

Vladi made a show to look at her and then back to Johnson. "Seems to me like she has a good understanding of how to have sex."

Johnson launched himself at Vladi, who easily side-stepped his attack, because he'd been expecting it. Unfortunately, at this very moment an American officer walked down the aisle outside the compartment and said with an angry voice, "What the hell are you doing on our train?"

Shit. Vladi bit his tongue and said with an even voice, "Sir, I'm very sorry for the inconvenience, but due to a recent surge in illegal contraband we have to inspect every person passing through our territory."

"The hell you do. I'm done with you rabble-rousers harassing our people. You have no business being on one of our military trains. Now get off or I'll arrest you for violating the sanctity of American property."

Why did the Americans always have to be so rude and aggressive? To Vladi it clearly showed that these imperialists had a skeleton in their closet. An innocent person with nothing to hide wouldn't put up such a fuss just because they were asked for their identification.

"I'm bowing to the threat of violence, because we Soviets are peaceful people," said Vladi and beckoned for the policemen to follow him. There'd be a French train to harass later in the day.

5

VICTOR

He had spent a wonderful day sightseeing with Bruni. In fact he'd never had so much fun with a woman, although she was totally not his type, because he usually preferred the more serious, intelligent woman to a shallow social butterfly like her.

But much to his surprise Bruni had turned out, if not intellectual, at least street-wise and with a huge heart for her friends, and – most important of all – she'd kept him rolling over laughing with her dry remarks and devil-may-care attitude.

After a delightful day, she'd invited him to a party she was hosting for a friend of hers, and had even assured him he'd go completely unnoticed in the crowd of American, British and French soldiers invited.

How could he have said no to such a charming invitation? Now he stood in front of the mirror at the barracks, shaving, and puzzled over why the cabaret singer affected him so strongly. It wasn't primarily her stunning looks, or her mysterious ways, but she appealed to him on much deeper level, which he didn't understand.

Another soldier entered the guest dormitory. "Richards?"

"In here," he called from the bathroom.

"Sergeant Victor Richards?" the other man asked.

"Yes, what's up?" He didn't look around, because he'd just set the blade to his throat.

"General Harris wants to see you."

Me? What could he possibly want from me? "Certainly, let me just finish shaving and I'll be out in a sec."

"I'll wait for you in the dormitory."

Victor finished shaving, wiped off the lather and freshened his face with cold water, before he entered the dormitory and put on shirt and jacket over his undershirt. "Ready to go."

"Okay, I'll bring you there."

Victor didn't ask for the reason and after walking several minutes across the compound they reached General Harris' office.

"General Harris." He saluted and stood at attention.

"At ease," Harris said and beckoned for Victor to sit down in front of the huge desk. "You're probably wondering why I called you here."

"Yes, sir."

"I hear you're returning to Frankfurt via train tomorrow morning?"

"Yes, sir. That was the plan."

"Well, we've just had some troubling news coming in.

The Russians have taken to boarding our military trains and harassing our personnel, claiming there are smugglers amongst them."

"Sir?" Victor could not believe his ears, although after the shenanigans Kapralov had pulled off at the ACC the day before, he didn't discount anything.

"They accuse us of violating the Potsdam or whatever else agreement to deflect that this is exactly what they're doing. Only the devil knows what they hope to achieve with this. I am placing military police on all wagons and have ordered them to prevent Soviet military from boarding our trains. In any case, I want you to be alert on your journey tomorrow and radio my office the very instant Soviet soldiers board your train."

"Yes, sir. Anything else?" Victor hoped to be dismissed, because he had an appointment with Bruni to keep.

"Once you have returned to Frankfurt, call me and give me a detailed report about what has happened, even if nothing has happened."

"Yes, sir."

"You may leave now. It seems you're in a hurry."

Victor hadn't thought to be so obviously desperate to get going and now felt his ears burning. "Sorry, sir, but I have been invited to a party."

"A woman I suppose?"

Victor nodded.

"Just be careful, because most of them only care for your wallet, which is not a bad thing in itself if you don't stupidly fall for their scheming and expect true love."

"Understood, sir." Victor was here for only two days; he

41

certainly wasn't dreaming about a happily ever after. No, his idea of a future wife was a girl from back home in rural Montana who cooked well, knew how to ride a horse and wasn't above hard manual labor. None of those traits fit the glamorous singer he had a date with.

Half an hour later he walked into the Café de Paris, which was closed for the day to everyone except Bruni's guests. The moment he saw her platinum blonde hair and that smashing body, he smiled.

She spotted him and waved him over, her long fingernails painted in brilliant red. "There you are. I was afraid you'd bail out on me."

"I would never do that," he said, wondering what would be the appropriate way to greet her.

"Good decision," Bruni giggled and took his arm.

"May I ask what this party is about? Someone's birthday?"

"No. It's a farewell. One of my best friends is leaving for Wiesbaden."

"Wiesbaden? That's right next to Frankfurt," Victor said.

"How nice. You might meet up once she's there. She's a bit shy, you know, and it would certainly help if she already knew someone over there."

Victor furrowed his brow. Was Bruni trying to match him up with her friend?

"Come, I'll introduce you to her." Bruni grabbed his hand and pulled him after her. "Hey, Zara, this is Victor Richards, he's stationed in Frankfurt am Main."

"Pleased to meet you," Victor said and eyed the beautiful long-legged woman with waist-long ebony hair, pale skin and vivid red lips. For some reason the image of Snow

White begging the hunter for her life sprang to his mind. Maybe it was because of the timid and vulnerable expression in her beautiful eyes.

"It's all my pleasure," she said with a soft, silky voice that didn't quite match the hard German accent, and offered him her hand, even though she looked like a frightened deer that would rather run away.

Bruni tugged at his sleeve and continued to introduce him to more and more people. Minutes later his head whirled with names and faces. Zara, Marlene, Laura, Heinz, Lotte, Patricia.

He had difficulties remembering all the names, but he gathered that Heinz was the nephew of the man who owned the Café de Paris and Laura's boyfriend, while the other girls all seemed to be friends with each other.

Apart from Bruni's German friends, the place teemed with French, American, and British soldiers. Booze flowed freely and soon the atmosphere became frisky and boisterous. He quite enjoyed himself and barely noticed how the time flew by and people left the party.

"I came to say goodbye," Zara said.

Victor observed with astonishment how Bruni embraced her friend like she never wanted to let her go again. He'd never have thought her to be so truly attached to someone, not by the way she'd flirted with any and all of the men in the room that night. She'd given everyone her playful and charming attention, making everyone feel appreciated and wanted – including himself – without ever giving away a single glance into her soul. But now he saw true sadness in her eyes. It endeared her even more to him.

Once Zara had left, most everyone else bid their goodbyes, and when only a handful of Bruni's German friends were left, she whispered in his ear, "Do you want to come with me for a nightcap?"

Victor hadn't been actively looking to get laid this night, but now that Bruni offered, he wouldn't say no.

6

DEAN

Dean was fuming. Sergeant Richards had reported back from his train journey that the Soviets had been acting up again.

He knew it wouldn't change anything, but he still filed a formal complaint with General Sokolov and made it clear that no Soviet soldiers would board another American train. He didn't have to wait long for the retaliation.

"Get me Major Gardner," he barked at his secretary.

She was used to his temper and didn't even flinch as she said, "Yes, sir."

Five minutes later Major Jason Gardner entered Dean's office. "You wanted to see me?"

"I swear, if I ever meet Sokolov in a dark alley, it will be the end of him!"

With one look at Dean's irate face Jason grasped the gravity of the situation and asked, "What has he done this time?"

"That SOB has closed the railway lines and Autobahn

connecting Berlin with our zones. Who does he think he is?"

"The Soviet Kommandant of Berlin," Jason said dryly.

"Ha ha. Very funny." Despite his foul mood Dean couldn't help but smile. Jason was his sounding board and grounded him whenever the pressure piling up on top of his shoulders became unbearable.

"Did the Russians give a reason?"

"Apparently this is due to technical difficulties. Technical difficulties, my ass! That's pure power play, because we don't let their filthy men search our trains."

"And did they give a timeline?"

"Oh, come on, you know as well as I do that the Russians never give timelines and if they do, they never stick to them."

"One can always hope…" Jason settled into the chair in front of Dean's desk.

"Sorry…I didn't offer you a seat."

"Glad that I never wait until you do."

Dean appreciated his friend's attempt to lighten his mood, but he was immensely worried. "You know what this means, don't you? In one fell swoop, our dear friends have essentially stopped the movement of troops and supplies into Berlin."

Jason rubbed his chin. "We can still fly in the supplies we need for our garrison, it's really not that much."

"Good idea. We'll do that, but we shouldn't accept their feigning of technical difficulties just to harass us. I mean, for the past weeks every time we changed our trucks and trains to meet their requirements for letting us use the Helmstedt Autobahn and the railways, they have changed them the next day. They've used one feigned excuse after another to block the traffic, pretending the need for some urgent repairs. And every time they reopen one part of the Autobahn, they close down another one that apparently was in bad shape, or they find a bridge that's not safe to cross over. And you know what's the epitome of brazenness?"

"No, what?" Jason leaned back in his chair, knowing full well he shouldn't interrupt Dean's rant right now.

"Now they claim that the bridge across the Elbe at Dessau needs repairing and therefore no more traffic is allowed in or out of Berlin to the Western zones. Do you know who built this bridge less than three years ago? We did. Our army engineers did. And I'll drag every single one of their asses in front of a court martial if the bridge they built doesn't even last three years!" Dean was getting short on breath. He was fed up with Sokolov's antics, but unfortunately there wasn't much he could do short of threatening him with a new war.

And thanks to the appeasers in his own government even this wasn't an option. The blockheaded politicians at home simply didn't understand that the only language the Russians understood was strong-arming them the same way they did us.

Jason looked at him patiently and Dean came down from his raging high. "I wonder what they want to achieve?"

"It could be a test."

"A test for what?" Dean asked, even though they'd talked about this before.

"Our determination to stay in Berlin. And…finding out whether we're able to supply our garrison by air."

"Damned right we are!"

"It's a rehearsal for the big thing we all know is coming." Jason was calmness personified as usual, but Dean knew that behind the nonchalant exterior his friend was as angry as he was.

"The Russians know as well as we do that there's no way to supply an entire city by air. This is a warning. They want us to see how futile it is to resist and how vulnerable we are."

"You're probably right. I'm sure they'll lift the traffic restrictions in a week or two and then Sokolov will show up at the Kommandatura with some outrageous demands, insinuating in his not-so-subtle way that we're at their mercy."

Dean didn't respond, because Jason had voiced his greatest fears. He'd been thinking about this for a while and had secretly been stocking up on provisions. Apart from food, which was mostly provided by the neighboring states of Brandenburg and Mecklenburg, both of them part of the Soviet-occupied zone, the most important provision was coal.

Coal was used for heating, cooking and electricity – both private and industrial. Without coal there would be no life in Berlin. According to the Potsdam Agreement, stone coal was provided by the Ruhr area located in the British zone. From there it was transported via train or barge to Berlin. Importing the coal by truck was impractical and flying it in by air impossible.

Right now, the city had a supply of twenty-one days of coal – a mere three weeks before they had to capitulate to the Soviets, should those make good on their evil threat.

"From your mouth to God's ears!" Dean said, scratching his chin.

"We won't be able to rely on God alone."

"No. I want you to work out a plan with the logistics unit to stock up on basic provisions. Flour, potatoes, canned meat, and coal. I want trains loaded with supplies waiting at the border and pushing through as soon as the Russians lift traffic restrictions. We need to make use of every single minute of unrestricted traffic they give us."

"You do know that this won't do much more than buy us a few days in an emergency."

"I know, worrywart. But I'm going to fight tooth and nail to defend our position in this heap of rubble. And now get working!"

"Aye, sir!" Jason stood and left the office, leaving Dean pondering his options should it come to the worst. There weren't many. Capitulation to the Russian whims and leaving Berlin – over his dead body. Flying in supplies via air and holding out long enough to find a diplomatic solution – he snorted at the hilarity of the thought. Forcing their way through the Soviet zone with a ground army... While he personally favored the last approach, he knew America was war-weary and even if General Clay supported the approach, they first had to get approval from the blockheaded appeasers in Washington.

He really was between a rock and a hard place.

But for the moment he had more urgent topics to attend to. A currency reform had to be prepared and the Russians couldn't get wind of it.

7

BRUNI

Bruni had just finished washing up the breakfast dishes when a knock sounded on her apartment door. She wasn't expecting anyone to visit this early in the morning. Looking down to her stockinged feet and her fluffy dressing gown – a gift of Dean's – she called out, "Who is it?"

"Me, Marlene."

Naturally her friend would be the only person to dare visit her at this ungodly hour when all decent people were either at work or still in their pajamas.

"Coming," she shouted back and took the heavy key from the hooks. After fumbling with the lock, she finally flung the door open and then smiled at a disgruntled Marlene, standing in the hallway on the other side of the door.

"It's about time," Marlene groused.

"Sorry. Come in. Why aren't you at university?"

"Because it's lunch time, if you haven't noticed."

50

Marlene's gaze wandered down Bruni's figure and she raised her brow. "How can you not be dressed at this time of the day?"

"Because I just finished breakfast, and by the way, it's my prerogative to stay in my dressing gown until I leave for the club. It's not like I'm receiving visitors here."

"And what exactly am I?"

"You? You're not a visitor, you're just a friend."

"Just a friend?" Marlene said with mock exasperation.

"Okay, my best friend, and for you I'd open the door even if I were stark naked."

Marlene scrunched up her nose. "Oh, please. Spare me the thought and reserve that for your lovers."

"Talking about lovers." Bruni led Marlene into the kitchen and offered her a sweet bun. "It's more difficult than I thought. It seems that nowadays all the officers bring their wives with them."

Marlene carefully chewed her bun before she answered. "Don't tell me you'll have to put up with a mere enlisted man. Wouldn't that be a cruel and vicious twist of fate?"

"I'm not that desperate. Time's on my side." But in reality, it wasn't. Bruni's supplies were running low and from her salary as a cabaret singer she couldn't afford the lifestyle she was used to. As much as she hated the idea, she'd have to tighten her belt. She eyed the rest of the sweet bun in Marlene's hand. From tomorrow on she'd eat bread for breakfast and only indulge in sweet delicacies at the club when an admirer paid for them.

"So why did you come here?" Bruni asked.

"Being your true undiplomatic self?" Marlene chuckled.

"Since you didn't call in advance, I gather you have some important news to share."

"You know me too well. Indeed, I have fantastic news." Marlene looked at her with barely concealed enthusiasm.

"Let me guess? Werner called you."

Marlene's face fell. She'd been in a star-crossed relationship with a high-ranking functionary of the Communist Party who'd had to cut all ties with her to keep her safe. "What makes you think that?"

"Because I heard him on the radio. He's now working for the American radio station in Wiesbaden."

"Oh. Good for him. But there's no way we can ever be together. Not unless the Soviets give up their grip on Germany."

"Which is as likely as hell freezing over," Bruni said. While she couldn't understand why Marlene had tied her heart to a man and still grieved for him after such a long time, she felt sympathy for her. But any advice she could offer would fall on deaf ears. Marlene simply didn't want to accept the truth that there were more than enough men in Berlin, and it didn't do any good to cling to the one who could never set foot in this city again.

"So, what's the good news?"

"We finally did it."

"Did what?"

"The members of the city council have ordered the Magistrat to open up a new, free and democratic university in the Western sectors of Berlin. This is huge. We won't be subjected to Communist indoctrination and Soviet harassment any longer."

"That's a relief." Bruni remembered all too well the arrest

and torturing of two student leaders the year before. "When will the inauguration take place?"

"By the end of the year, just in time for the winter semester. We'll call it *Freie Universität Berlin*, Free University of Berlin. We'll implement a progressive concept called academic self-government, and the cornerstones of our philosophy will be academic freedom and democracy."

"Just keep a stiff upper lip and don't get into trouble with the Russians until then."

Marlene sighed. "I certainly know better than to arouse their scorn."

"Why don't we go out to celebrate?" Bruni said, deliberately forgetting her vow to live frugally from now on.

"I'm sorry, but I don't have any money."

"Don't be silly. It's on me."

Marlene protested feebly, but didn't need much convincing. Someone who lived on ration cards was always hungry, and the prospect of having a proper meal in a restaurant that catered predominantly to Allied soldiers was too much to resist.

"Let me get dressed in a jiffy," Bruni said and disappeared into her bedroom. She put on nylon stockings, a dress, high heels, grabbed her purse and headed back into the kitchen.

"You look fantastic!" Marlene complimented her.

"There's never a time to let your hair down." Bruni knew she was vain, but her good looks were her capital and since she was still on the prowl for a new benefactor, she had to look extra good.

Marlene rolled her eyes and looked down her own formerly emerald-green dress, which had lost its brilliance after being washed a thousand times and now featured a greyish color with patches everywhere.

Together they left the apartment building and walked down the street.

"What about that Victor guy?" Marlene suddenly asked.

Bruni was taken aback by the question, since she thought she'd been very discreet. "What about him?" she asked more harshly than she had intended.

"Feeling guilty, are we?"

"Not at all." Bruni tried her best to give a nonchalant look, but Marlene broke out into laughter.

"You know you're a real bad liar?"

"Me?" Bruni raised her eyebrow, although she knew there was no way to deceive Marlene. "Okay. I admit it, he's a very handsome guy, but I thought I'd hidden my attraction for him quite well."

"You probably fooled everyone else at the party, but not me. The way your eyes were shining every time you looked at each other was the giveaway. I've never seen you that... happy...in love."

"I'm certainly not in love with him, I just found him attractive." Bruni avoided love like the plague. Not since the first man she'd ever loved had shattered her belief in humanity. Not even Marlene knew about that dark secret in Bruni's life.

They turned a corner and came to a stop in front of a queue of women handing bricks down from one of the buildings in ruins and throwing them onto a truck.

"I'm so glad we don't have to work as *Trümmerfrauen* doing this hard labor," Bruni said.

"Me too. My roommate Lotte did this for several months and she said it was an agonizing job."

Bruni looked at her manicured fingernails and felt slightly sorry for the women doing men's work. But then, everyone forged his or her own destiny. If these women couldn't be bothered to find an easier job, it was their own fault.

"You're evasive," Marlene said and cut through her thoughts.

"Me? Why?"

"Because normally you're gushing with all the sordid details about your lover's performance."

"Since you never want to hear them I may have decided not to bother telling you," Bruni said, walking around the working women.

"Liar. You never spare me the details."

"Nothing happened, so no details to speak of." Bruni felt herself blushing, which was absolutely outrageous for her. She never blushed.

"Oh my." Marlene slowed down her pace and looked straight into Bruni's eyes. "You're truly in love."

"I'm not." Bruni protested with some fervor, as if her friend had accused her of some sinister crime. "In case you forgot with whom you're talking, I'm Brunhilde von Sinnen. I don't fall in love. And he doesn't fit my criteria. Even if he did, he's based in Frankfurt am Main, so there's no way I'll ever see him again."

"Such a shame, because the two of you made a real nice couple. And the way he devoured you with his eyes. He was clearly as smitten as you are."

"I'm not smitten." They had finally reached the restaurant and Bruni welcomed the distraction of the waitress warmly greeting her. Back in the days when she was Dean's mistress, she'd often come to this place.

"Fräulein von Sinnen, we didn't know you were coming. A table for two?"

"Yes, please."

They ordered and indulged in a hearty meal while they gossiped about everyone and his dog.

"Say, your roommate Laura, how does she get along with Heinz?" Bruni asked.

"I don't like him, he's creepy."

"Creepy? Is he a pervert or what?"

Marlene wiped her mouth with a napkin. "No, not in that way, but he's shady. I'm pretty sure he's involved in illegal activities."

"You can be so naïve, Marlene. Tell me a single person in Berlin who doesn't skirt the law from time to time." Bruni took another bite of the potato casserole.

"*I* don't." Marlene's eyes twinkled with indignation.

"Oh yes, please forgive me, I forgot that you're Saint Marlene."

"I'm no saint, but I study law."

Bruni laughed. "Studying law is no reason to starve. So what criminal activities does Heinz engage in? Maybe he can be useful sometime?"

"Don't pretend you don't know; his uncle is the owner of the Café de Paris."

"Haven't seen him engaging in any illegal activities, but I might make a wild guess." Bruni didn't have to guess, because she was pretty sure Heinz's business was smuggling and black marketeering. Her boss was the uncrowned king of Berlin. He could get anything and everything, provided someone paid in foreign currency. And his nephew was the man in charge of sourcing the goods. Herr Schuster and Heinz both had the best connections to members of all four occupying powers, and most shady deals in the city went over their desks.

They finished their meal and Bruni kissed Marlene good-bye. "Thanks for coming by. Take care!"

Then she returned home and readied herself to go to the cabaret.

8

VICTOR

June 1948, in the middle of nowhere

"Damn this place," Victor looked into his empty beer glass with bleary eyes. His head swayed as he raised it and looked around the small room where he was the only one of half a dozen men drinking off their asses.

He'd been in here drinking for most of the night and the bartender had just announced the place was going to close in half an hour, but Victor wasn't ready to leave yet. He needed another drink. Another way to forget this godforsaken hole where he'd been locked up for the past two weeks.

When he'd accepted his superior's offer to devise the logistics of secretly delivering the new German currency into every corner of Western Germany except for Berlin, he hadn't foreseen this would mean being held like a prisoner in an isolated house on the American air base in Roth-westen, about ten miles north of Kassel.

He shared his isolation with only one other American soldier, the twenty-six-year-old First Lieutenant Edward Tenenbaum, son of Polish Jews who had emigrated to America. Tenenbaum was also an economist who'd graduated from Yale University summa cum laude.

He wasn't a bad fellow, but Victor always felt inferior to intellectuals, since he'd never finished his college degree. Apart from Tenenbaum, his only company was eleven German currency experts. The entire project was kept top secret – so secret the Germans had dubbed it *Conclave of Rothwesten*, referring to the College of Cardinals electing the Pope.

Apart from the participants, only the highest brass of the three Western Allies were privy to the events inside the cursed building. Not even the guards knew exactly what and whom they were guarding.

Victor cursed his bad luck and often wondered what exactly his role was in this illustrious circle. It wasn't that his German was especially good – in fact it was a lot worse than his already bad French – or that the scientists asked for his advice on logistics when quibbling over rules and regulations for the currency reform.

His only consolation was that he'd come late to the party and would have to endure this utter boredom and isolation for only two weeks instead of the seven like everyone else.

He thought back to his buddies, who'd be partying in Frankfurt or Wiesbaden right now, celebrating the demobilization of yet another bunch of them. Turnover was fast these days and most everyone who wanted was sent stateside again. Oh, how he yearned to go home. He'd take a nice, long vacation on the farm of his parents, find himself a good old-fashioned girl to marry and then move with her to a town with a small airport where they needed a man with engineering skills. He'd buy a small house with a yard, settle down, and soon enough three children would arrive. There, he'd forget all about the war and Germany.

That's what he wanted. Being drunk only made that longing worse, and he felt a stab in the chest thinking about his parents. He hadn't seen them in such a long time. Another wave of homesickness settled over him and he sighed forlornly.

"Hey, buddy," the American cook, doubling up as bartender in the improvised bar, said. "Time for you to go to sleep."

Victor nodded, staggering to his feet and heading for the exit, his steps clumsy as he bumped into several tables before finding his equilibrium.

The next morning, he woke with a pounding head to the disturbing news that an important visitor had announced his arrival.

Shoot. Of course this had to happen today of all days, when Victor was in less than presentable shape. He strode into the bathroom at the end of the hallway, his long legs eating up the ground quickly. An ice-cold shower quickly returned the life to his body. After dry-rubbing his hair, he wrapped the towel around his hips and stepped in front of the mirror to shave.

Dressed and ready, he settled down in the mess that doubled as a bar at night to have breakfast, and almost choked on his cereal when General Harris strode in.

Victor jumped up from his seat and saluted him.

"Please, continue your meal," Harris said and sat down at Victor's table.

Just great!

"How's everything going?" Harris asked.

"Sir, I'm only here to offer advice on logistics; the real experts are the Germans."

"I know, but..." Harris lowered his voice, even though there wasn't anyone else in the room. "We might need a Plan B."

Victor was befuddled. "Yes, sir. Anything I can help with."

"We have learned of the Soviet efforts to introduce their own new currency in their zone."

"That was to be expected," Victor said. Nobody could expect the Russians to sit back and wait. The greatly devalued Reichsmark was doomed to die either way and the Russians wouldn't let sovereignty over the currency out of their hands. In fact, they'd stubbornly insisted that printing German money was their exclusive privilege and should only be done in their facilities in Leipzig – which was one of the reasons why the Reichsmark had inflated so fast. At this point, cigarettes had become the currency of choice and the only thing thriving across the four zones was the black market.

"We also believe their currency reform will include Berlin."

That was a game changer, as the Western allies had meticulously excluded the capital from the scope of their own currency reform – mostly to avoid another clash with their Soviet partners.

"Would the Russians really be brazen enough to defy us in such a bold way?" Victor asked. "After all, Berlin is under quadripartite rule."

Harris gave a wry cough. "They're cutthroat liars, thieves and mobsters. Of course they will be brazen enough. But we will be prepared."

"Yes sir." Victor said, although his hungover brain couldn't quite follow the train of thought. And he wondered why Harris was telling this to him and not to someone else.

"I have ordered the printing of the letter B on two hundred fifty million Deutsche Marks and getting them into Berlin, just in case."

Victor shook his head. "That's a helluva lot."

"Seventy tons to be exact."

"We can't possibly transport that much by either train or truck into Berlin, without the Russians getting suspicious. Who knows, they might even close the Autobahn again, just to get into our hair."

Harris smiled. "That's why I came to ask you – I hear you're quite the expert in air logistics."

Shivers ran down Victor's spine when he realized the magnitude of what Harris was suggesting. "That would be at least ten planeloads. If we don't transport anything else" – he squinted his eyes at the general– "but probably the only way. The Russians have no means to inspect our aircrafts. Not in Western Germany and not in Berlin. But we would have to make sure nobody at Tempelhof airport knows. The Russians have their spies everywhere."

"I have had the same thought. What do you suggest?"

Victor was in his element. He grabbed pen and paper

from his breast pocket and drew a few boxes. "How many boxes do you think?"

"Depends on the size."

"Of course. I was thinking about small wooden crates that we use for liquor."

"Liquor?"

"Yes, they are quite sturdy, and it's only natural that they would be separated from the rest of the supplies."

"Good thinking. In fact, we could leak to the Russians that our supplies are running low because of their shenanigans and we're restocking alcohol and tobacco supplies just in case of further technical difficulties on the road."

"They must think us a bunch of alcoholics," Victor said.

"Believe me, they won't even flinch. Vodka is a sacred liquid for them and running out of it is akin to a state crisis. By when can you have the complete logistics plan ready?"

"If this is my top priority I can finish by tonight, but," Victor looked at the general, "it would be good if I could have a look at the actual money stacks. Or at least know the exact amount and how much space it takes up."

"You know that this project is top secret and nobody who's involved can leave Rothwesten before the currency reform has been implemented?"

Victor nodded, thinking of another way he might get the required information, when Harris spoke again. "Nobody without security clearance, that is."

"Sir?"

"You'll be flying out to Frankfurt in one hour. There you'll be confined to the security barracks until all of this has been accomplished. Better get packing right now."

"Yes, sir. May I ask one question?" Victor emptied his mug of coffee.

"Go ahead."

"Won't the Soviets retaliate if we outfox them like this?"

Harris nodded. "You can count on that. They'll cry bloody murder and accuse us of every crime under the sun. They might retaliate in unexpected ways. It might even provoke the final clash."

Victor swallowed. But General Harris seemed to be cold-blooded enough not to have a single care about what the Russians might do. Victor saluted and left the room. Within the hour he'd been transferred from one prison to another one. But at least in Frankfurt he could do something useful, instead of sitting here with the scientists who never asked for his opinion anyway.

9

BRUNI

Bruni's husky alto voice rang out as she sang the final bars of her chanson about lost love. The cabaret was full tonight and she'd taken her time during her set to scope out the available men. Most were regular customers, Allied soldiers of all four occupying powers.

Personally, she didn't discriminate against one nationality over the other, but since she lived and worked in the French sector, she'd recently kept a careful distance from Soviet soldiers. In case the palpable tensions between the Allies exploded and it came to the much-feared rupture and the end of quadripartite rule, she wanted to be seen as a loyal supporter of the French.

On the other hand, she certainly didn't want to rebuff the Russians if the worst-case scenario came to fruition and the Western Allies left Berlin to the Soviets. So, she walked a fine line, doling out her favors in carefully measured doses.

Maybe it was a good thing that Dean had dumped her. If

worst came to worst, the Russian NKVD would feast on the American Kommandant's mistress. She shuddered involuntarily and her voice squeaked higher than it was supposed to. She quickly composed herself. It wouldn't do any good to show signs of distress. She was simply a singer, a woman with no political ambitions and no idea of international diplomacy.

Finishing the song, she spied Capitaine Pierre Lejeune sitting at his usual table and when he winked at her, it immediately bolstered her mood. Pierre wasn't good-looking by any means with his beaked nose and sparse dark hair. He was way beyond fifty years old, much too old for her.

"That was wonderful, Bruni," Herr Schuster, the owner of the Café de Paris, said as she exited the dressing room and headed for the seating area.

"Thank you," she replied with a nod. Naturally he was more pleased by the champagne that was ordered during her performance than by her singing. He was a bulky man in his late forties with brown hair, dark brown eyes that seemed to observe everything, and a thin-lipped mouth. She didn't especially like him, but he was okay to work with. He never bothered the girls working for him and didn't let his hands wander as so many other bosses did.

For that she was thankful, although he gave her a slimy feel anytime she was forced to converse with him, because it was all too obvious how he really made his money. It certainly wasn't selling booze to the soldiers who frequented his club. Behind the scenes anything and everything was up for sale. It was an open secret that Herr Schuster could fulfill every wish and organize every luxury, if the recipient paid enough – and not in devalued Reichsmark.

Despite her disdain for him, she secretly admired his guts. In fact, she and he were very much alike: both of them catered to the dreams of the occupying soldiers and neither of them discriminated against any one nationality.

"That Captain over there asked for you to join him for a drink," Herr Schuster said.

"I'll sit with him for a while, Herr Schuster."

"And inveigle him into having a meal, maybe? There's fresh caviar from the Crimea."

"I'll do my best." Bruni danced away. Caviar was one of her favorite delicacies, and since she was running low on money and supplies, it was a double treat to eat at the club.

She smiled at Pierre and took the chair he held out for her. She'd not seen him at the club for a few weeks and pretended to pout. "It's been too long since you last graced me with your presence."

Pierre didn't take the bait and answered pleasantly, "I've been very busy. We all have been. Besides, I was supposed to return to France on leave yesterday, but our dear friends have interfered with my plans." He glanced across the room and bowed his head in a slight movement at one of the Russian officers sitting at the bar.

"What have they done this time?" Bruni said and suppressed a peal of laughter, since she'd heard that very expression so many times from Dean.

"Just blocked the Autobahn again for technical reasons."

Bruni shook her head. "How come they can't maintain one stupid Autobahn for longer than a few days at most? Even when the Englishmen and Americans bombed the heck out of our country, we never once closed the Autobahn."

Pierre put a hand on hers. "Don't tell me you're that naïve, Mademoiselle Magnifique. We all know it's an excuse for harassing us."

Bruni smiled and softly removed her hand from under his. She wasn't stupid, but she'd made it a rule not to talk about politics ever with one of the soldiers. It was a conversation where a German girl could only lose, especially when she wanted to stay on the good side of all four powers. "So, you're staying in Berlin instead?"

"I am. And I might appreciate agreeable company that keeps me from despairing." He gave her a very saucy look.

On second thought, Captain Lejeune might not be such a bad catch. He wasn't married and had agreeable manners – although the other girls in the club had often complained about his exotic preferences in bed. Bruni wondered just how exotic they were. She would have to ask Carla before she made a decision she might not be happy with.

"I'll have to check the roster," she said noncommittally. "You know how Herr Schuster is with us girls."

"Then I'll see you tomorrow night and await your answer," he said and kissed her hand.

She got up and saw how one of the whores settled on his lap and the two of them engaged in heavy smooching, only to leave the club a few minutes later in a close embrace.

No, Pierre definitely wasn't for her. She didn't mind her man having a wife somewhere back home, but if he couldn't wait a single day and shoved off with a whore mere minutes after she'd given him a decisive maybe, he wasn't for her.

Bruni put on her megawatt smile and crossed the

cabaret, flirting with all the men in her path, before she returned backstage to retouch her makeup for her last performance that night. Back up on the stage, the image of a certain American engineer with dirty-blond hair and gray-green eyes wouldn't leave her mind and she put all the bottled-up emotions into her song, singing exclusively for him – wherever he might be right now.

She didn't understand herself, because it wasn't at all like her to pine after a man, and an unsuitable one at that.

10

DEAN

June 15, 1948

D ean was sitting in his living room with his wife, a glass of whisky in his hand, when suddenly the peacefulness of the night was disrupted by the sound of breaking glass. A large brick with a note wrapped around it landed a few inches from his feet.

"Dean!" his wife gasped in shock.

"It's okay. Go sit with the boys, just in case the noise woke them up."

"What are you going to do?"

"Probably nothing. I'll take a look outside but I'm guessing I won't see anyone." He waited until she had left the sitting room and then he unwrapped the brick, inwardly wincing at the blatant threat contained therein. It was one thing to receive death threats at his office, which was a fairly standard occurrence.

But this was different. This was his home. The place where his wife and sons should be safe from the effects of his job. He tossed the note into his briefcase and then located a spare board and a few nails and boarded up the window until morning.

He turned down the lights and checked all of the windows and doors on the ground level. Before joining his family upstairs, he retrieved his pistol and some extra ammunition.

As much as he loathed doing so, he might have to ask for his private residence to be protected by American soldiers. He knew where the death threats, the anonymous calls and the thrown bricks came from. Die-hard communists, Soviet stooges who believed they could scare him enough to leave Berlin.

But they had reckoned without their host. He'd never leave Berlin to Stalin's sycophants. Although he now wished he hadn't brought his family to Germany. It had been a purely selfish move, because he'd missed them so much, even though they'd been a lot better off back home in the United States.

After a sleepless night, Dean dragged himself to the obligatory meeting in the Kommandatura. There weren't many things in this world he loathed as much as his nemesis General Sokolov.

To his utter dismay he found out that Sokolov had added

another urgent point to the agenda, the worrisome bleeding out of Berlin's industries to Western Germany.

"Sanctimonious prick," he said to his deputy Jason. "After stealing everything that's not nailed down from under our asses and shipping it to the Soviet Union, he's worried about bleeding out the industry in Berlin?"

The reparations demanded by the Soviets were a constant thorn in Dean's side, even three years after the end of World War Two. But this was a completely new angle to the issue and he had to give Sokolov credit for coming up with ever more ridiculous accusations.

As expected Sokolov barely waited until the current chairman, French General Ganeval, had officially opened the meeting, before he stood up and began one of his feared insult-laden monologues.

"Last year, thirty-seven industrial complexes have been robbed from the Berlin people and sent to Western Germany in a clear violation of the Potsdam Agreement."

Dean leant over to Jason and said, "Since when does our friend here care for written agreements?"

Sokolov droned on, "Among them are such illustrious names as Karstadt, Knorr-Bremse, Kodak and Singer sewing machines."

The vein in Dean's neck was pulsating furiously and he interrupted the Russian, "Singer is actually an American company, and you're the ones who robbed their machinery in violation of the Potsdam Agreement even before we arrived here."

Sokolov's face twisted with pain and Dean felt a surge of *Schadenfreude*, because he knew the other man was suffering from ulcers again.

"This is imperialist propaganda and defamation of the great USSR. May I remind you that we bore the brunt of the fighting in the Great Patriotic War, while you stood idly by and fought a few unimportant proxy wars in the Pacific, instead of going up against the Nazis."

Dean preferred to keep silent. Even though Sokolov's accusations were grossly exaggerated, they weren't completely unfounded. The United States had waited much too long to enter this war, erroneously clinging to the idea of isolationism. He still couldn't get his head around the fact that most people back home had believed America could stay out of this "European war".

Nowadays the world had grown together in a way that every country – with the exception of some tiny and backwards island groups in the Pacific – was interwoven with everyone else through trade, politics and immigration.

In any case, it didn't do any good to argue with Sokolov. Just like the isolationists at home, the Soviet general had a set point of view, no doubt directly derived from the *genius* Stalin, and wouldn't change it even if it meant the end of the world.

Jason leant over and said, "Has it occurred to the Soviet economic geniuses that these companies are leaving Berlin because they fear being dismantled by the Russians? Or that they need functioning police who don't arrest and kidnap every worker who criticizes the Soviets?"

"The Americans are despicable in enabling the blatant theft of production material. We know that you're smuggling out not only industries, but also art, jewelry and other valuables in your military trains. In the Yalta Conference it was stipulated…" Once again, Dean was speechless at

Sokolov's brazenness. How could they refer to whatever conference whenever it suited them, twist the meaning of the agreement, and then completely forget it ever existed when it didn't fit into their scheming ways? "...Something must be done against the shameless plundering of German property by the Americans." Sokolov ended his speech on a high-pitched accusation.

Now Dean was truly worried. Even though he was used to abuse by the Russians, this had sounded like an open threat.

Thirteen hours later the Kommandatura meeting was deadlocked. Not a single agreement had been reached, not even for the most trivial issues like the color of newly issued ration cards.

Dean closed his eyes as exhaustion pulled at him. A glance at the clock on the wall told him it was already midnight. After Sokolov's accusation that the Americans had robbed Berlin of its lifeblood, the discussion had returned to the *"Fourteen Points to Ameliorate the Legal and Material Positions of the Workers of Berlin"* – a pamphlet they'd relentlessly discussed for the past six months without being able to agree on anything.

"If the Soviets rescind Order No. 20, we can then resume discussions of the fourteen points individually," General Ganeval, the chairman, declared, not for the first time.

Without Kommandatura approval, the Soviets had issued this order in their own sector, making all fourteen points law, which in itself was a violation of the much-cited Potsdam Agreement. If Dean were the current chairman instead of Ganeval, he'd tell the Soviets what exactly he thought of their criminal activities. But Ganeval was much too suave to confront Sokolov in such a direct manner.

"The fourteen points must be accepted in their entirety," General Sokolov declared emphatically, his face twisted with pain.

It was the same circular argument that had been going round in this room for the past months. The Soviets insisted on their all-or-nothing position, knowing full well the Western Allies would never agree. Their Order No. 20 was only the last drop to show the other allies how little the Soviets cared about their opinion.

The end goal was clear: sole rule over Berlin, Germany and ultimately Europe.

"We will not rescind our lawful order unless the other delegations agree to the fourteen points and issue an agreement that shall stand for the whole of Berlin," Sokolov declared, sitting back in his chair after his statement and staring at the others in the room with disdain in his eyes.

That did it! Dean was peeved. Thirteen hours of constant abuse and no end in sight. Add to that a sleepless night because of a death threat against his family – no doubt orchestrated by the despicable Russians – and the fact that he had an important meeting the next morning... He decided to leave the meeting. It was a mere formality and had been done before.

"I'm out of here," he whispered to Jason and then stood up and addressed the company. "Gentlemen, I'm afraid I must excuse myself. I have a heavy schedule tomorrow and it's getting very late. With your permission, Chairman Ganeval, I'll leave my deputy Major Gardner in charge."

Chairman Ganeval nodded. "By all means. Major Gardner, please take General Harris' seat as representative of the American delegation."

Dean nodded once and then left the meeting room. He stepped into his waiting car and told the driver to take him home.

11

VLADI

Vladi glanced anxiously at General Sokolov. What would he do now? Harris had set the stage with his rude walking out of the meeting, clearly showing how little the Americans cared about their other allies.

Stalin wanted the other occupying powers out of Berlin, because they were a constant threat to the safety of the Soviet Union. Their only reason to stay on was Berlin's location in the middle of the Soviet zone, which gave them an ideal position to spy on the Russians and to advance their secessionist plans for the rest of Germany.

Everyone knew that the British and Americans hated the Russians for their guts and their better economic system that was so far superior to the predatory capitalism in their own countries. Now they wanted to bring Germany on their side and then attack the Soviet Union when she least expected it.

In Hiroshima and Nagasaki the Americans had shown their true colors. They had no respect for human lives and had used two nuclear bombs to flatten entire cites including hundreds of thousands of civilians – men, women, and children.

Since the Soviet Union still didn't have her own nuclear bomb, she was vulnerable to the imperialists' vicious thirst for land. Big Capital had started the aggression and forced the Soviets to fight the Great Patriotic War against the Nazis, and nobody, except for the war-mongering Americans, wanted another war.

Vladi stood fully behind any measure Sokolov could take to put the enemy in their place. Otherwise, the Soviet Union would soon cease to exist.

Sokolov stood up. "General Harris' behavior is an affront against our delegation. There are procedures to be adhered to and I refuse to tolerate the atrocious conduct of this American hooligan."

The room fell silent. Vladi thought Sokolov was being slightly theatrical. Harris had committed a shameless act by walking out on the other members of the Kommandatura, but he hadn't acted violent or atrocious.

General Ganeval, conciliatory like the Frenchman always was, took floor. "I can adjourn the meeting if you so wish, General Sokolov."

Sokolov winced as if the other man had punched him in the guts and turned a dark shade of purple. "I will not reward such an insult to the honor of the great Soviet Union. General Harris has to be called to account for this!" He took a short pause and then continued with a droning voice: "Since the rest of you won't stand up for decency and honesty, you're complicit with the beastly Harris. If Harris doesn't return and excuse himself immediately, I will not remain here anymore." With these words he proceeded to move to the door.

Vladi let out a breath. It was done. He grabbed his papers, stuffed them into his briefcase and made to follow Sokolov. It took a few moments until the translator had finished translating Sokolov's words and the Russian delegation had already reached the door when General Ganeval spoke up.

"In fact, General Harris has been properly excused from the meeting, leaving his deputy in place. But you, General Sokolov, are walking out without permission on no more grounds than throwing a hissy fit over supposedly being stood up."

Vladi knew that Ganeval was right, but that was only a technicality. What mattered was Harris' intention to humiliate the Soviet delegation.

Tomorrow the newspapers and the radio would tell the Berliners the true story behind the walkout. How the Western Allies had behaved like the cheating and lying hoodlums they were and forced the Soviets to walk out on them, the way a mother might walk out on her toddler throwing a temper tantrum.

What Vladi didn't understand was how Sokolov planned to go on from here. After Marshal Kapralov's walkout from the Allied Control Council a few months earlier, the Kommandatura was the only four-power council left. Wouldn't it be tiresome to rule Berlin without it? Or did he hope the Western powers would come crawling back with an apology? Unlikely. They could be stubborn at times.

～

The next morning Dean was summoned to General Clay's office.

"You have done a terrible thing," the general greeted him.

Dean and Clay had not always been on the best of terms, especially during the early days after the war when Dean had been the only warning voice about the disastrous policy of appeasing the Russians.

But the general must have a certain appreciation for him or otherwise he wouldn't have made him Kommandant and promoted him to Brigadier General. Still, Dean was resolved to remain silent and wait for what his superior had to say.

"And you know what's the worst about all of this? You're not even sorry!"

"You are damn right I'm not," Dean snapped, forgetting his determination to stay silent. "The Russians have terminated quadripartite rule over Berlin on a whim. What else can they do now? How can they continue to shower us with their abuse? Personally, I am relieved. It was about time they showed their true colors and stopped this farce that the Kommandatura has become. As far as I'm concerned, they have done me a favor and ended a veritable nightmare. And you know what? It was premeditated. They were just waiting for a reason to dump us. And since they have become desperate to finish off four-power rule, they grabbed the flimsiest reason they could find. That the American Kommandant left the conference room after being properly excused by the French chairman."

Dean had to stop his tirade to catch his breath and Clay took the opportunity to interrupt him. "While I may agree with you on a personal level, this doesn't excuse your actions. The Soviets will most certainly retaliate. In fact, I received a written complaint from Marshall Kapralov, saying that after your vicious destruction of German unity, Berlin loses its importance as the location for the Allied quadripartite administration. In his letter he insinuated that the Western Allies should go packing."

Dean grunted. A reaction like that had to be expected. He just wondered whether the politicians at home would grant the Soviets their wish. But thankfully General Clay assuaged his worries and affirmed that nobody had any intention of leaving Berlin.

They had paid dearly for this heap of rubble, and they would stay.

12

BRUNI

June 20, 1948

Bruni was sitting on the shore of Wannsee Lake watching Marlene and Lotte splashing about in the water like small children. She shrugged and turned her face so the big-brimmed straw hat cast a shadow on her face. Despite the heat, she made sure the silk scarf around her shoulders didn't leave a single inch of skin uncovered.

Only farmhands and silly women like her friends exposed themselves to the sun and received an inelegant tan. She stretched out her long, nylon-covered legs and, much to her chagrin, noticed a run creeping up her stockings. That would keep her busy for hours mending it.

The battery-powered wireless by her side was playing American music from her favorite station, RIAS Berlin, when the program was suddenly interrupted by the news that on the hour, General Clay would make an important announcement to all Germans in the three Western zones.

That was highly unusual, and she waved wildly at her friends to make them return to the beach.

"What's up, Bruni?" Marlene asked as she took the offered towel.

"There'll be an important announcement by General Clay."

"What could be important enough to merit such an unusual move?" Lotte mused.

"I don't know, but I guess we'll soon find out." Bruni shrugged. "By the way, have you received news from Zara? I expected her to write as soon as she's properly installed in Wiesbaden."

Marlene shook her head. "You know how unreliable the mail is. Sometimes it takes a while."

"Three months?"

"Good heavens! Has it been that long? I've been so busy with work and studies..." Marlene made a face and Bruni knew that her friend was feeling guilty for not being more on top of things. She herself had had a nagging feeling that something was wrong for the past weeks but had always pushed it away, telling herself that Zara was as busy as everyone else and hadn't found the time to send a letter to her friends. Which was very unlike her.

But it had been better to cling to that idea than to worry herself to death about Zara's fate, when there was nothing Bruni could do about it.

"She's grown up, she can take care of herself," Lotte said. "And besides, what could possibly happen to her in Wiesbaden? It's not like the Russians can roam free over there and abduct people the way they do here."

"Yes, I'm sure she'll let us know she's fine as soon as she finds some time," Marlene said, but the worry was etched deep into her face.

The radio announcer interrupted their discussion. They listened to the introduction of a new currency called the Deutsche Mark into the so-called *Trizone* consisting of the American, French, and British zones in Germany, with the exception of quadripartite Berlin.

Bruni yowled, "Why not us?"

"Because of the Russians, what else?" Lotte answered. "They must have opposed it."

"I'd drop dead to the ground, if they even knew about the currency reform." Marlene leaned back to look at the others.

For a moment Bruni was perplexed. Rumors had abounded for months, though nobody had known anything for sure. But the four allies surely had coordinated their efforts.

Lotte, who always knew more than everyone else, said, "Why do you think the occupation currency wasn't worth the paper it was printed on?"

"Because of the inflation." Despite not being interested in politics or economics, Bruni wasn't stupid.

"But do you know why we had this inflation? Not because there weren't enough things to buy, but mostly because there was too much money."

Bruni smirked. "Now you're kidding me, Lotte. There can never be too much money, at least not for me."

Both her friends laughed at that remark and Marlene

started coughing from laughter. When she had calmed down again, she said, "Not for you, but for the economy as a whole it's bad when you have plenty of money and few goods. It starts a death spiral of inflation and soon people don't buy and sell goods for devalued money, but barter instead or use a surrogate currency like cigarettes."

Lotte explained further, "Anyhow, all four occupying powers owned a set of original plates to print occupation currency. And while the three Western Allies used austerity in printing money, the Soviets sped up the printing presses to fulfill their every wish, thus severely devaluing the currency."

"Oh." Bruni had never thought about it that way. "So... you're saying...since they behave like the reckless fools they are, the other Allies deliberately kept them out of the currency reform?"

"Yeah. I have heard rumors that they insisted the Deutsche Mark should be exclusively printed under their supervision in the printing facilities in Leipzig. Apparently, the other Allies were not amused..." Marlene giggled. "... and preferred to continue their plans without the Russians, especially following Marshall Kapralov's dismantling of the Allied Control Council back in March."

"But what will happen to us?" Bruni asked.

Lotte answered with a serious face. "Nobody knows. Berlin was kept out of the new currency to appease the Russians, but we all know how well that worked in the past three years."

"There will be retaliations," Marlene added.

"That...you can bet your ass on. Girls, we are in a hurry now. We must return home and exchange whatever money we have for cigarettes and other in-demand goods." Bruni might not have a thorough understanding of economics but she sure knew how bartering worked.

"How can you be so cunning?" Marlene said in shock and Lotte added, "Do you always think only about yourself?"

"Actually yes, because I want to survive. What about you?" Bruni did not want to argue with her friends about the skills needed for survival, since not even her best friend Marlene knew about her devastating childhood.

After being abused by her father for years, she'd run away from home at the tender age of twelve. Living as an urchin for a year and barely surviving from day to day, she'd vowed never to be poor and vulnerable again.

She patted her hair, thinking about how far she'd come since she'd left the gutter and taken control over her life – something she wouldn't give up ever again. Not for a man, and certainly not for quarreling Allies and their childish power struggles.

13

VLADI

June 22, 1948

Geneeral Sokolov was livid and had summoned his entire staff to an emergency meeting. His face was an even deeper shade of purple than usual and he was downing copious amounts of warm milk with honey to soothe his ulcers.

A single glance at Sokolov's irate expression chilled Vladi's blood, because he feared Red Army Intelligence would be made the scapegoat for the disaster unfolding in front of them.

They had been as surprised by the currency reform as the German citizens, since even their best spies had known nothing at all about it. He wondered whether he'd be simply demoted or sent to a gulag, because, no doubt, consequences would follow.

With sweating palms, he took his seat in the huge meeting room across the hallway from Sokolov's office. The room reeked of history. Only three years prior they'd celebrated the German capitulation in this very room and raised their glasses to everlasting friendship with their Western Allies. But ever since, the shady imperialist thugs had done everything to undermine the friendship, harm the Soviet people, and usurp power over Germany, culminating in this final secessionist act where they'd shoved a new – illegal – currency down the throats of the unsuspecting citizens in their zones.

Sokolov opened the meeting. "From day one, the Americans have worked against German unity, because for their plan of world domination to work, they need a weak Germany. They haven't shied back from hurting the people, stealing their means of production and shipping it across the Atlantic Ocean to be rebuilt in their own country! This is an affront against freedom and democracy in the world and a violation of the brotherly spirit they promised to foster in the United Nations."

Vladi looked around the audience. Everyone nodded eagerly. Was he the only one to know that no production means had been shipped from Germany to the United States, but on the contrary the Americans poured plenty of money into the war-devastated European countries?

When he caught the eyes of a political advisor to Stalin, he nodded too. Truth or no truth, he didn't want to end up in a gulag for not agreeing with the official Soviet directives.

"The *Bizone* was the beginning of a sinister plan to tear Germany apart. After blackmailing the French to join them and form the *Trizone*, they now have finished their dark work: The Western Allies have forced Germany apart. With their illegal currency flooding our zone there's no way back. In fact, we must close our borders to protect the bleeding out of goods and industries in our quest to ensure the economic welfare of not only the Germans, but all of our communist brother nations in Europe."

Vladi swallowed hard and listened to the immediate actions to be taken. First of all, the Soviet military administration would issue a law declaring possession of the Deutsche Mark illegal. Anyone found carrying the illicit currency would be subject to arrest and severe punishment.

That was actually a good sign, because if Sokolov issued that kind of order, he needed the help of the NKVD and Red Army Intelligence to implement the draconian punishments envisioned.

But the plan was more sinister than this, because Sokolov enquired of Colonel Ulyanin, the commanding officer of the Soviet air force in Berlin, whether the Americans would be able to provide food and medicine for the city by air.

"Comrade General," Ulyanin said, "as we have seen in our test run earlier this year, the Americans and British are indeed able to supply their garrisons with all provisions needed. We believe they are able to uphold air support for an indefinite time."

Sokolov pursed his lips. "I am not asking about their garrisons, Comrade Ulyanin. My question was whether they will be able to provide food and coal for the civilian population in their sectors."

The entire room fell silent. Vladi stopped breathing, and

it seemed everyone else had done so, too. The only sound one could hear were the birds chirping in the luscious gardens surrounding the SMAD headquarters. Seconds grew into an eternity, and he did not envy Colonel Ulyanin for having to give such a momentous answer.

"Comrade General, I believe, this is not possible," Ulyanin said with a shaky voice.

Sokolov's face beamed. "Then it will be done. Start preparations for a blockade."

Three days later, Marshal Kapralov announced over the radio that a new East Mark would be introduced to Berlin. He concluded the announcement with the following words: "Effective immediately, Berlin is no longer quadripartite, but has become an economic part of the Soviet zone."

"God, no," Bruni murmured. She sure as hell didn't want to live under the Soviet thumb, because three years after the end of the war, it was clear as crystal that the Western zones prospered, while the Soviet zone languished.

What she knew from her Russian admirers was that the Soviet people lived in abject poverty, longing for completion of the revolution in a not too distant future. Because then, they'd finally have enough food, clothing and proper accommodations to live comfortably.

She did not doubt that every small bit of progress in the German economy would first benefit the Soviet Union. Only when tens of millions of people had been lifted from poverty would any progress be made in Germany. By then she'd be old and ugly.

Not her choice.

Bruni walked to the kiosk at the corner to buy a copy of the communist newspaper *Neues Deutschland*, where Kapralov's announcement had made it prominently onto the first page. Back in her apartment she read the entire article and became more worried with every word.

The American, British and French occupation authorities have introduced their secessionist currency reform against the interests of the German people, in the attempt to fulfill the wishes of the American, British and French monopolies eager to weaken Germany, to dissect it and to enslave its workers. This has resulted in imminent and severe danger for the reconstruction of Germany and developing a peacetime economy. Therefore, we find ourselves forced to implement immediate measures to safeguard the interests of the German people.

Bruni groaned. Since when did the Soviets care for anyone's interests except their own?

First, starting tomorrow, June 24th, 1948, a new currency will be introduced in the entire territory of the Soviet occupied zone, including the area of Greater Berlin. The new bank notes are based on the Reichsmark notes with glued-on stamps to distinguish them as new money.

Second, they are the sole permitted denomination in the Soviet occupied zone as well as in the area of Greater Berlin.

Third, every citizen, factory, organization and office in the Soviet occupied zone and the area of Greater Berlin is obliged to exchange all old currency for the new one by June 28th, 1948.

Fourth, after June 28th, no institution, shop, agency, or person will be permitted to use the old currency.

. . .

Bruni took a sip from her coffee and let the newspaper sink into her lap. Every single article in the entire paper was about the currency reform. And every article was full of the usual accusations against the Western powers, capitalists, Wall Street, Nazi criminals, speculators, bankrupters, and whoever else was not a communist.

Marshall Kapralov declared a strict prohibition on using the new German Mark in Berlin and issued a hidden warning to the other Allies as well as to the general population if they didn't obey. His exact words were "The SMAD will use economic and administrative sanctions to make sure every person uses nothing but the new East Mark."

Bruni shuddered. She assumed Kommandant Harris and his garrison would laugh at Kapralov's threat, but people like her lived in fear of a *social visit* from the NKVD. Until now she'd thought herself safe, because the NKVD officers were as vulnerable to her charms as every other man, but maybe that had been wishful thinking.

No, she would definitely not live under Soviet occupation, because the memory of her years in the gutter were too deeply imprinted in her memory. If the Western Allies pulled out of Berlin, so would she. She loved Berlin dearly, but she loved her life more.

Bruni sat down to write a letter to Zara, asking about her well-being, life in Wiesbaden and opportunities for Bruni to move there. In the afternoon she walked to the Café de Paris. Everywhere she passed, people were talking about one topic: the currency reform and the counter reform. It impacted every single person in Berlin, and nobody was quite sure what would happen next.

The people in the Soviet sector usually drew the shortest

straw, but in this special case, they were the lucky ones. There was no room for error, no decisions to make. They would simply obey their masters, exchange their money and hope to live another day.

Whereas Bruni was left with doubts. Should she go ahead and exchange her few remaining Reichsmark into East Mark as ordered by the Russians, or should she wait out and hope for the Western Allies to bring their Deutsche Mark to Berlin?

Since the deadline for exchanging was four days from now, she decided to wait and see. But then she had a better plan and on her way to work passed by the black market to buy cigarettes, which was a lot harder than she'd thought. None of the black marketeers were willing to accept Reichsmark.

Apparently they were waiting to see what the higher powers decided and changed their cigarettes only for US dollars, British pounds, French francs or the most coveted currency of all: precious metal.

The whole situation was getting unpleasant, but there was nothing Bruni could do. For now, she walked to work, where the other girls were excitedly chatting about the bombshell Marshall Kapralov had flung onto Berlin.

"Did you hear?" Gabi said.

"Hear what?"

"Everyone who is found in possession of Deutsche Mark is considered an enemy of the German economy and a traitor to German unity."

"Russian propaganda." Bruni weaved her way through the chattering girls to sit down in front of the huge lit-up mirror. "The Deutsche Mark has been distributed only in the Western zones of Germany, not in Berlin. At least I haven't seen a single note so far."

Sally, who had three small children at home and a missing husband, furtively glanced around before she said, "My brother just returned from Hamburg and brought some notes with him. He said they'd serve us better than the Reichsmark."

Bruni closed one eye to stick on false eyelashes. "Before long, the Deutsche Mark will arrive here and everyone will accept them, just like they accept dollars right now. Not officially of course, but all the under-the-table dealings will be done in the new currency. I, for my part, will hold out on exchanging my Reichsmark."

Gabi had already exchanged all her Reichsmark at the designated bank and proudly showed them the old, worn Reichsmark note with a thumb-sized violet stamp with a wavy, white fringe, the number ten for the denomination and 1948 for the year.

Each denomination had a different colored stamp: blue for the one Mark, light green for the two Mark, and so on. All of the girls, most of whom hadn't exchanged their own money yet, were curious to see the new banknotes and passed them from hand to hand.

"Oh no!" Gabi suddenly cried out.

"What's wrong?" Bruni asked.

"Look! The stamps are peeling off." Gabi was disconsolate and Bruni wondered why she made such a fuss. "At the bank they told me if the stamp is somehow tampered with, damaged, or falls off, the banknotes cease to be valid." Gabi broke out into tears. "Oh my God! Give me back my money! Right now! I have to fix this!"

Bruni felt for her, but couldn't help feeling satisfaction that she herself had taken the right decision in waiting things out. Once the Soviets saw how lousy their stamps were, they'd think of a better way to mark the banknotes. As long as this didn't happen, Bruni would know better than to exchange her Reichsmark for a new currency that disappeared into thin air, simply by touching it.

"I'll wait to exchange my Reichsmark," Sally said and voiced what all the girls in the room thought.

"What's going on here? Why aren't you ready?" Herr Schuster poked his head inside the dressing room. "We're opening in half an hour and neither the kitchen nor the bar is staffed. What are you girls gossiping about? Hush, hush, go to work."

He was gone as quickly as he'd come, and the kitchen workers and waitresses quickly followed him to get the cabaret ready before the first patrons arrived.

Bruni walked over to the coatrack and chose a shimmering silver gown with a pink feather boa for her first performance. Herr Schuster wouldn't have any sorrows with the currency reform, since his clients normally paid in hard foreign currency. And about a year ago he'd stopped accepting rubles, claiming it was illegal to do so. Which in fact, it was, but his real reason was that the ruble was even more worthless than the devalued Reichsmark.

14

DEAN

June 23, 1948

Dean was talking on the phone with Sergeant Richards, who assured him Plan B had worked like a charm and two hundred fifty million Deutsche Mark, stamped with a B in blue indelible ink, had made their way safely into the warehouses in Berlin.

"Sir, the banknotes are ready to be distributed whenever you wish," Richards said.

"I appreciate your hard work. It was a mammoth task."

"Thank you, sir."

"If you're ever looking for a job in Berlin, let me know. We're always in need of good aviation engineers."

"I'm honored, sir, but I'm quite happy in Frankfurt and looking forward to returning stateside. Have been wanting to return to college and finally get my degree for a long time."

Dean ended the call. Sergeant Richards was certainly one of the best men in the Engineer Aviation Battalion and had a greater understanding of airport logistics than anyone else Dean had known. It was a mystery to him why the man was still a sergeant.

He decided to dig deeper into Richards' personal file, because if there was a skeleton in the closet to explain this peculiarity, he wanted to know what it was.

Dean's deputy knocked on the open door.

"Come in, Jason. What's up?"

"Nothing much." Jason grinned. "Sokolov's spitting mad about the currency reform and is now shoving his worthless Wallpaper Marks down everyone's throats."

"Wallpaper Marks? Where did you hear that?"

"On the streets. You know how the Berliners are, dubbing anything and everything with irreverent sobriquets. The East Mark notes are quickly losing the glued-on stamps and people are reluctant to use them."

Dean laughed. "Better for us."

"I hear Sokolov's ulcers are killing him and in revenge he's been sending military staff to Siberia by the trainload."

"Serves them right." Dean was done with pretending to be civil. Should the Russians eat each other alive, he wouldn't shed a single tear. "We knew this would happen. Whoever owns the money, owns the economy. They couldn't let us get away with this."

"Actually, I didn't come here for chit-chat," Jason said.

"Not? And here I thought we could hold a *Kaffeeklatsch* to brighten our day." Dean picked up his cup of coffee with pinky finger daintily outstretched, pretending to be a fine lady ready for her daily coffee-and-cake gossip.

"Your French and British counterparts will be here at ten hundred for an emergency meeting. Do you want me to stay on?"

"No, I'll give you a call if I need you."

"Okay, I'll get to work then."

Jason left the office and Dean mused for a few moments how to bring the other two men on his side. His British colleague Lieutenant General Otway Herbert wouldn't be a problem, but the Frenchman General Jean Ganeval was always eager not to infuriate the Soviets. Still, even the French must have realized that ship had sailed long ago.

Quadripartite power was history, and now it was vital to reconcile the remaining three. Otherwise they wouldn't stand a fighting chance and the Russians would haul their asses out of Berlin before the others could blink.

"Good morning gentlemen," he greeted them an hour later and cut right to the chase. "We need to rethink our decision to leave our sectors in Berlin out of the currency reform."

"You are aware that this will most likely cause retaliation by the Soviets?" General Herbert said.

"It will be akin to a declaration of war." That answer might be a bit dramatic but was to be expected from Ganeval.

"The last thing any of us wants is another war, but are you willing to cede economic domination to the Soviets? If so, we should all pack up and leave Berlin tonight." Dean stared at the other men as they digested his last statement. "We can't stand by and watch how they shove the worthless

East Mark down everyone's throats with the threat of arresting anyone found accepting or in possession of our Deutsche Mark."

"As always, the Soviets are playing rough," said the Brit.

"I'm more than ready to play rough, too." Dean certainly had had enough of the Russian antics. "If you don't agree with me, I'm willing to go alone and introduce the Deutsche Mark solely in the American sector."

It was a concealed threat, because the others knew how impractical this suggestion was; for the action to be successful it was either none or all. They needed to show a united front, not only to the Soviets, but also to the Germans. Dean was certain that the very moment the Berliners doubted solidarity among the three Western Allies, they'd lose hope and defect to the Russian side with flying colors for the sake of their very survival.

After a short discussion his two collogues agreed and when the argument turned to the practicalities, Dean put his trump card on the table. "I happen to have two hundred fifty million freshly printed Deutsche Marks, identified with a B sign, in my warehouses and we can start distribution by tomorrow."

There was nothing else to say.

15

BRUNI

June 24, 1948

B runi walked home from the cabaret and arrived at her apartment in the wee hours of the morning, tired and with aching feet. Singing and dancing all night in six-inch heels had become second nature to her, but braving the pothole-filled streets of Berlin in the same high heels wasn't an easy task.

She unlocked the door and flipped the switch to turn on the lights, but nothing happened. With a muttered curse, she groped for the flashlight she kept on the shelf by the door for these occasions. The electricity supply in the city was sketchy at best.

She slipped out of her high heels and wiggled her hurting feet, while heating the gas stove to make coffee –

real coffee. It was already twilight outside and she switched off the torch to save on the batteries.

Waiting for the water to boil, she switched on the battery-powered radio and fell backwards into the chair when she heard General Sokolov's gnawing voice announcing that due to the illegal currency reform in the Western zones and the resulting bleeding out of goods into the capitalists' hands, the Soviet administration had been forced to close all streets, railroads, and waterways connecting Berlin with the Western zones.

"Dirty son of a bitch!" she yelled, picking up her shoe and throwing it at the radio. Luckily for the device, she missed.

But the announcement wasn't over yet. A radio news reader explained that due to technical difficulties, the delivery of electricity from the Zschornewitz power station in the Soviet sector to the other sectors had been interrupted for an indefinite amount of time. The speaker continued without a trace of emotion in his voice. "During the traffic interruption it won't be possible to supply Berlin's Western sectors from the surrounding regions, a part of the Soviet occupied zone. According to the Potsdam Agreement each occupying power has to provide food and coal for their own sector."

"Murderous bastards! Do you want to starve us all?" Bruni was about to launch her second shoe at the poor radio when the kettle whistled. At least they hadn't cut off the gas – yet. With a glance at the clock she decided to drink her coffee, forego sleep and visit Marlene, before her friend left for class.

Obviously, the electric doorbell didn't work, but since

the front door at Marlene's apartment block had never been fully repaired, it took only a well-placed punch against the lock to open it. Bruni trudged up to the third floor and knocked on the door.

After a while she heard a shuffle and a sleepy voice asked, "Who's there?"

"It's me, Bruni."

The door opened and a rumpled-looking but also very worried Marlene waved her inside. "What's happened to you? Why are you up so early?" It was only natural for Marlene to be worried, since Bruni never made social calls before noon. Everyone knew how sacred Bruni's beauty sleep was.

"I never went to sleep. And this is what happened." She flipped the light switch in the small hallway.

"The electricity is out again. But surely this isn't the reason for you to come here at," Marlene yawned and glanced at the clock in the living room behind her, "five thirty in the morning."

Bruni rolled her eyes. "You have no idea! Haven't you listened to the radio?"

"If you haven't noticed, I was fast asleep until some obnoxious woman knocked on the door about one minute ago," Marlene said with a slightly dour face, and Bruni couldn't help but giggle. She didn't feel very sorry either, because this was a nice revenge for all the times Marlene had torn her from slumber at different ungodly hours in the morning.

"I wouldn't have come if it weren't important. It's not a normal outage. The Soviets have cut off electricity to the

Western sectors, and they've closed down all transport ways between here and the Western zones in Germany."

Marlene seemed too sleepy to understand the enormity of Bruni's words and shrugged. "They've done this before, nothing to get all upset about." Then her face took on a suspicious expression, "What aren't you telling me? Did you plan to travel to the American zone? Because of that GI, what was his name? Victor?"

Victor had been the furthest thing from Bruni's mind this morning, but she couldn't prevent a slight flush and a warm feeling when the image of his face entered her mind. Though she wouldn't tell Marlene.

"He has nothing to do with this, and just for your information, I'm completely uninterested in him. He was a nice distraction, nothing more. He can't give me the lifestyle I want and by the way, he's stationed in Frankfurt and I'm living in Berlin. So whatever relationship you're cooking up in your mind, there's nothing, and I mean nothing at all, between me and him in real life."

"Quite a few words to say no." Marlene waggled her eyebrows and for whatever strange reason Bruni felt caught red-handed, even though there really was nothing between her and Victor and he really was completely unsuitable.

"Back to the reason I came here," Bruni said as matter-of-factly as she could, shoving away all yearnings for Victor. "This time it's for real. This is their retaliation for the currency reform. Sokolov said in his speech that they were forced to close the borders because of profiteering and smuggling."

"They are the ones doing most of the smuggling."

"I know, but mark my words, this is their opportunity to

rid themselves of the despised Western Allies and incorporate all of Berlin in their stupid communist empire."

"That actually is a frightening prospect," Marlene said, with a shiver.

"We'll all be doomed." Bruni sighed. "They explicitly said providing the Western sectors with food would not be possible while the *interruption* is in place. Their goal is to starve us all. More than two million people."

"Now you're exaggerating. The Russians wouldn't do that; we're not at war anymore," Marlene said, but the expression on her face betrayed her fears.

"Seems like Zara has been ahead of the game. She always knew it's best not to tangle with the Russians. What do you think, should we make plans to leave Berlin?" Bruni surprised herself with these words. She crazily adored her city and had never wasted a thought on leaving this place, not even during the horrible aftermath of the war. And certainly not now when conditions had slowly started to improve.

Marlene shook her head. "I grew up here. It would be hard to leave. Let's hope things will calm down. Nothing has been decided yet."

"From your mouth to God's ears!"

In the afternoon, RIAS Berlin brought the news that as of today all citizens in the three Western sectors of Berlin could exchange their Reichsmark for the new Deutsche Mark, stamped with a B. Both the Deutsche "B" Mark and the East Mark were legal tender within the area of Greater

Berlin.

Bruni grabbed her entire stash of Reichsmark. This time the decision was easy, and she hurried to the nearest bank to exchange her money for the new Deutsche Mark. Then she got ready for work, surprised to find Marlene at her doorstep when she made to leave.

"What? Now you believe me?"

Marlene blushed. "I'm sorry. You were right. But it's much worse than we thought this morning. The British retaliated and stopped all freight traffic from their zone to the Soviet zone." That was a biggie, because both the Hamburg harbor and the Ruhr coal industrial area were located in the British zone and the Soviets depended on the high-quality black coal to power their industries.

"I have to go to work, coming with me?"

Marlene nodded and they linked arms. "Are you sure the Café de Paris is even open? I mean, most of the public transport, factories, shops, and offices have closed today due to a lack of electricity."

"The Café has a generator, and I'm sure Herr Schuster has the means to get enough diesel fuel to run it...after all, his clientele are Allied soldiers."

"At least General Clay has said on the radio that the Americans plan to stay in Berlin."

"That's a relief." Bruni said, "And looking at the bright side of it, I'll bet that Dean is regretting bringing his family here and dumping me for them."

Marlene stared at her with wide open eyes. "You don't honestly believe the Russians are doing this to avenge you?"

Bruni giggled and shook her head. "No, of course not.

I'm not that self-absorbed, no matter what you might think about me."

"I didn't say…"

"I know you didn't," Bruni teased her. "But you have to admit, it's a nice thought."

"Wouldn't be the first time a war was started over a beautiful woman."

"Should I call myself Helena?" Bruni giggled as she thought of the myth about the beautiful Helen of Troy.

16

DEAN

For two days Dean barely left his office. He was in constant phone conversations and personal meetings with his superiors, the air base in Wiesbaden, and his colleagues Generals Ganeval and Herbert. This was the defining moment everyone had awaited with anxiety. All talks with the Soviets had ended a few days prior with their bold move to put an entire city under siege.

The Moscow thugs didn't flinch at the prospect of starving two point two million people with their traffic blockade and announcement that no food would be supplied from the Soviet occupied zone into the three Western sectors of Berlin.

"Rotten rats!" Dean cursed in a rare moment when he wasn't talking on the phone. Jason, who'd taken up residence in his office, didn't even lift his head at the expletive. He was bent over a huge map of Germany, using a felt-tip pen to draw the three agreed air corridors onto the paper.

"This idea is plain crazy," Jason murmured. "You and I both know it's impossible to supply a city of this size by air. There simply aren't enough aircraft in the world, let alone in Germany. And we have only two airports here, both on their last legs, if I may say so."

Dean got up from his desk and approached Jason to look over his shoulder. As always, Jason was right. It was pure folly without the slightest chance of success. The Soviets had been more than pleased with the results of the so-called milk run, because the "little" rehearsal airlift earlier this year had clearly shown the limits of supply via air.

Even if they managed to fly in enough supplies to feed the population during summer, this would abruptly end when autumn arrived and coal for heating was needed. Let alone the difficulties of landing aircraft in the city in bad winter weather.

Truth be told, an airlift was impossible. Everyone knew it, including the Soviets.

"Now everything makes sense." Dean suddenly saw with clarity the Soviet plan.

"Care to let me in on your revelation?" Jason asked.

"The reason why the Russians have been launching demands for all kinds of new air regulations is right here." Dean tapped on the map. "They have been planning this blockade long beforehand. Or why would they want every flight into the Berlin air space to be announced twenty-four hours before departure? Why did they suddenly insist on us obtaining their permission for every civilian flight? And why were they all at once so concerned about the noise level in Berlin that they suggested abolishing night-time air traffic altogether?"

Dean looked expectantly at Jason, who dutifully answered, "Tell me."

"There's only one answer to this. Since they can't blockade our aircraft in the air they want to make it next to impossible for them to touch down. This is their final move of squeezing us out of Berlin. And once they have the capital they'll go after Germany and the rest of Europe. Then it's only a matter of time before the Soviet empire attacks the United States on our own territory. We cannot allow this to happen." Dean knocked his fist on the table. "Sokolov will get me out of Berlin only over my dead body."

"I'm sure he wouldn't mind."

"He sure wouldn't. Do you remember them buzzing the British transport machine back in April?"

"I do. It was clearly an aggression from the Soviets and resulted in the death of both crews."

"It was a test to see how far they can go. In the end it was considered an accident, but any thinking person knows this is not true. It was a calculated maneuver to see how we'd react. They buzzed a British machine, knowing my friend General Herbert would be much more lenient than I."

"I honestly never believed the Soviets would stoop this low. I mean, what do they hope to gain by starving two million people? Surely they must be aware this is not the way to earn the trust and friendship of the Berliners?"

"Pah," Dean spat out. "Murderers, rapists and thieves. They could care less about the people in their custody. Stalin starved tens of millions of his own people by pushing through his stupid land reform in the twenties."

"What can we do?"

"We supply the city by air – for as long as we can. Every

109

single day will buy us time for diplomatic negotiations and move us one day closer to the resolution. I still hope there's some smidgeon of honor in Stalin's dark soul and we can come to a solution that doesn't involve two million dead civilians."

The city had ample stocks to feed the population for about three weeks, a precautionary measure taken after the forewarning of continued traffic obstacles. Dean counted on the fact that flying in more supplies would show the Russians how serious the Americans were in their decision to stay in Berlin, and that a diplomatic solution would be found well before the food ran out.

"General Clay has suggested using armed ground forces and fighting our way from Helmstedt to Berlin," Jason said.

"While I personally am quite fond of this solution, President Truman has completely ruled out such an undertaking. For now, the directive is to avoid another war at all costs, and sending ground troops into Soviet-controlled territory would certainly mean war. The airlift is the only way to postpone the choice between leaving Berlin with our tails between our legs and starting another war. Thus, we're back to square one. Show me what you have."

Jason as always had done the homework and had already talked to General LeMay, commander of the US Air Force Europe in Wiesbaden. "LeMay has promised us a dozen C-47 aircraft immediately and up to one hundred in a few weeks, should Congress approve."

"What about our allies?" Dean asked.

"I talked to Ganeval's deputy first and, as was to be expected, the French have neither men nor aircraft at their disposal. They're still heavily engaged in the Indochina war. But they have agreed to support us with logistics and supplies."

"At least that's something."

"Whereas the Brits are a lot more helpful. Herbert has already talked to his Prime Minister and has been given the green light to send daily twenty-four planeloads of supplies to Berlin."

"See? We're going to nip the Russian blockade in the bud. They'll give up before the week is over." Dean was a lot more enthusiastic than an hour earlier. Now he wanted to get a feeling for the mood on the ground. "Let's drive to Tempelhof airport, what do you say?"

"Aircraft spotting?" Jason chuckled. "We used to do this when we were kids. So, why not?"

Both of them grabbed their jackets and caps and off they went to watch the cargo planes land in Tempelhof. Despite the constant death threats, Dean refused to give up his open-topped jeep and as they drove through the city, German citizens recognized the car and shouted anxious questions at him.

He stopped quite a few times to assure them that they shouldn't worry, because the Americans were here to stay and wouldn't throw the Berliners into the paws of the Russian bear. But he could see that his assurances, while well-received, didn't disperse all their doubts.

When Jason turned on the radio to listen to the Soviet-controlled radio station, they found out why. The propaganda war was fully under way, and the station blared the most vicious terror reports about deadly riots in the streets of Berlin, looting, murder, and arson. All, of course, incited by Western troops who were shooting the German mobs at point blank range.

According to the Soviet radio, Dean wasn't able to drive to Tempelhof, because the streets were filled with hundreds of carcasses.

"Doesn't look like a riot to me," he said as he told his driver once again to stop at a crossing to give some words of reassurance to several gathered Germans.

As they drove on, the radio announcer proceeded to tell the most vicious of all lies. Apparently the American, British and French military were overwhelmed in dealing with the chaos in their sectors and fleeing the city head over heels, begging the Russians to expedite their departure.

"Can you believe this?" Jason asked.

"Sokolov will suffer for this! Those assholes really stop at nothing. They think if they spew enough lies, the people will end up believing their shit." Dean was shouting and the vein in his temple was pulsating dangerously.

"The Berliners are the most propaganda-hardened people I've come across. They didn't fall for the Soviet lies during the election campaign in '46, and they won't fall for it now either."

"At least that's something." Dean drew his brows together in a scowling expression. With every lie coming from the radio, he understood better that this was the real deal and not some rehearsal threat. Stalin had decided to kick the other Allies out of Berlin, cost what it may. Even the starvation of two million people.

When they jumped off the jeep at Tempelhof, an anxious

aide was already waiting for them. "General Harris, you're requested at the station commander's office immediately."

"I'm coming," Dean said and drew his brows together. Being summoned by the station commander was highly unusual, but what was normal these days?

"Sir, I'm so very sorry, but the station commander said it's of the utmost importance. Someone from the Office for Military Government in Frankfurt has called looking for you."

Someone from the OMGUS in Frankfurt? That was even more unusual. Clay resided in Berlin, and LeMay had already clarified details with Jason earlier this day. Who else could have such an important topic as to search for him all over Berlin?

"Probably someone from Rhein-Main airport peeved that we're flying in the supplies from Wiesbaden," Jason said. "You go and take the phone call and I'll wait for you down on the airfield."

"Okay." Dean followed the aide into the fifth floor of the airport building, where the commander resided.

"General Harris, it's Major Briggs for you," the commander said and handed Dean the telephone receiver. Major Briggs was the commanding officer of army troops in Greater Hesse and an old friend of Dean's.

"Hey, Robert, what's the hurry?"

"We've just heard the news on the radio and you can imagine how worried everyone is. Do you need troops to get the situation under control? I can rush them in right away, just tell me what you need."

So much for nobody believing the Russian propaganda. The Berliners might be immune, but his own army colleagues weren't. Nobody who hadn't lived in Berlin for an extended period of time remotely believed the shenanigans that Sokolov and his cronies constantly pulled. Whenever Dean visited a base in the American zone, people gave him that indulgent look, dismissing him as an exaggerator.

17

VICTOR

Victor was in the hangar and watched the people scurrying around the Rhein-Main airport, or Rhein-Mud, as the pilots had dubbed it.

Ever since the Soviets had started to blockade Berlin two weeks prior, the Rhein-Main and Wiesbaden airports had become two hotbeds of activity. All available pilots and transport machines had been ordered in from all over Europe and every day more machines and crews arrived at the already crammed quarters.

Rumors had it that an entire Navy flyer squadron from the Pacific would soon arrive, bringing with them their large C-54 aircraft, much bigger than the rather small workhorse Gooney Bird.

Victor had never been more thankful that he was only an engineer and not a pilot, because he sure as hell didn't want to participate in this folly of an airlift, called Operation Vittles. Most of the crew were fighter pilots with zero experience in air transport. Understandably, they were less than enthusiastic to exchange their sleek fighter planes for the clumsy Gooney Birds. For them, it was a rather boring mission to transport food instead of doing heroic dogfights in the skies.

Glenn, a newcomer whose reputation as a reckless pilot preceded him, walked up to Victor. "Hey, man, seen a bird I could use somewhere?"

Victor shook his head. In the rampant disorganization of the first weeks with new planes and crews coming in faster than they could be accommodated, the pilots were constantly competing with each other to find a machine that was fueled up and ready to go.

The same was true for sleeping quarters, where often two or three men shared one bunk, taking turns sleeping while the others were flying. The entire operation was a complete and utter mess.

"Quite the excitement. I love being in the air. I don't care what the mission or purpose is. Doesn't matter if it's just to Berlin and in a transport machine. It's all right as long as it's above the clouds." Glenn beamed with exhilaration. "What about you? Ready to go to Berlin?"

"Me? No way am I going into that shithole. The one time I was there was more than enough. Nothing but rubble." Except for a certain platinum blonde woman who had wormed herself into his soul and heart. Despite his best intentions to forget about her, she constantly popped up in his thoughts.

"Come on, can't be worse than Rhein-Mud. What do you say I take you one day as my crew engineer? I hear the Berlin girls are spectacular."

Victor inwardly cringed. How come these youngsters assumed that an engineer could do anything with engines? Victor's specialty was airport design, functionality and transport logistics. He had no idea how a plane worked and definitely couldn't fix a problem midair. "No thanks. I'd rather stay on the ground than set foot into one of those tin cans."

"Man, you have no idea what you're missing. I'm by far the best pilot around here," Glenn said with a proud wink.

"Yeah, I've seen your takeoffs and landings. I'll pass," Victor said. In his opinion they were all suicidal for voluntarily boarding these machines from hell, but Glenn was a special kind of reckless. He must have been the star in a flying circus in a previous life. Victor shuddered. If he had to fly, it surely wouldn't be with acrobatics-loving Glenn, but with an older, experienced pilot who actually cared for the well-being of his passengers. Glenn gave him a jaunty salute and sauntered off to find an aircraft.

If Glenn claimed to be the best pilot around, Victor certainly was the best airport construction expert. That's why his former commanding officer had lured him after the war to stay in Frankfurt am Main with the promise of a promotion and a free hand in rebuilding the airport. Neither thing happened, because his CO had died of a heart attack last year and the new one was the biggest asshole that ever occupied the earth – a man who didn't have the slightest idea about anything to do with engineering but had somehow made it to colonel in the Engineer Aviation Battalion while Victor himself still was a sergeant. He scoffed. The only one to blame was Victor himself. He should have asked for a transfer to another unit a long time ago.

Half-heartedly he'd finally put in his request for demobilization, which had been granted mere days before the rotten Soviets had pulled off their blockade. Naturally, the order had been revoked, as all hands were needed at Rhein-Main airport.

Another pilot jogged toward him. "Hey, man, have you seen a pallet with dry milk that I'm supposed to load?"

Victor pointed his thumb to the far corner. "Baby products are over there." Once again, he cursed his CO for not seeing the necessity of a streamlined logistics process to load and unload the planes. Everything could be so much faster with a well-planned process, but no, the asshole insisted on letting the pilots find their way.

They didn't even have proper guidelines for maintenance and spare parts. Whenever a machine limped home, the flight engineers frantically searched around for a spare part they could use. It didn't help that most of the machines were old and worn-out war birds that had seen better days and had been called back from their well-deserved retirement.

Victor sighed. Everyone had hoped that within a week or two, there'd be a diplomatic breakthrough, and the blockade would be lifted. But no such luck. Just a few days ago, General Sokolov had announced that unfortunately it was not possible to resume traffic between the capital and the Western zones.

Unfortunately, my ass! It was a calculated ploy for supremacy over Berlin and honestly, Victor didn't understand why General Clay didn't simply hand over the darned city to the Soviets on a silver platter. There was nothing but rubble there. Ruins, dirt, devastation and hunger. And Bruni's mesmerizing blue eyes. He shrugged it off. He didn't want to think about her.

18

BRUNI

Bruni squinted her eyes to glue on the fake eyelashes that had come loose during her last performance, a task made that much harder by candlelight. The small power stations in the Western sector worked at full capacity, but they couldn't replace the electricity that had been provided by Zschornewitz prior to the blockade. Therefore power was switched on only for two spots of two hours each, every day, rotating between the boroughs.

The cabaret had its own generator, but since fuel was running short, Herr Schuster had turned off the lights in all the rooms except for the kitchen. Even on stage, Bruni sang in a dim twilight, careful not to stumble down the platform in her high heels.

This blockade had turned out to be an awful nuisance in more ways than one, and it seemed there was no end to it. Many people had wanted to leave the city by now, but only those with relatives in the Soviet occupied zone had been allowed to. Everyone else without access to a plane was trapped inside the besieged city.

Bruni had neither.

During her performance she eyed the men in the audience. While there wasn't an explicit ban, the Soviet soldiers had been discouraged from entering the Western sectors; therefore she was quite surprised to recognize Red Army Intelligence Captain Vladimir Rublev.

She had to look twice, because this was the first time she'd seen him in civilian clothes, but it was unmistakably him. He might be able to fool the counter-espionage men, but not her, since she had an uncanny eye for faces and features.

Under different circumstances she might have considered him a great catch. He was rather good-looking in a rugged, sailor kind of way, with less than stellar manners, and a girl in every city. But according to the grapevine, all of his girls adored him and he never mistreated any of them.

He must be here on some clandestine business, but Bruni couldn't care less. This was her chance to get some inside information. After her song, she walked up to his table and settled beside Vladimir, pretending not to recognize him. "Hello, sweetheart, want to buy me a drink?"

He furtively looked around before he nodded and replied in accent-free German, "Why not?"

Bruni waved at the waitress and ordered champagne for both of them, musing about how to best broach the sensitive topic. When the champagne arrived and they both clinked glasses, she offhandedly remarked, "With the blockade going on, it's so hard to get stuff like champagne."

It was innocent enough, but would hopefully provoke him into giving away some information.

"Sugar, you shouldn't believe the Western propaganda. There's no blockade," Vladimir said.

She choked on the champagne and could barely suppress a coughing fit, before she regained control again. "I'm just a simple singer, but aren't the road closures for real?"

He indulged her with a smile, before he said, "The reality is that the Soviet Union has ordered all traffic between Berlin and the Western zones subject to Soviet inspections. A necessary measure to stop black marketeers and profiteers from draining valuable equipment belonging to Berlin's industry into the hand of the capitalists."

"I've heard a lot about smuggling, but I never knew the Americans were smuggling valuables into Berlin."

"They aren't. They're smuggling them out." Vladimir was getting impatient.

"Oh, I'm sorry, I got confused. So why are the Russians holding up traffic into the city and not out of the city?"

"We...they don't. But since the Western Allies defy all rules and regulations, the Soviets had to defend themselves. A temporary restriction of certain types of land transport can by no means be called a blockade, and the Soviets certainly aren't the bad guys attempting to starve two million West Berliners. In fact, it was the Nazis who besieged Leningrad for close to three years and starved hundreds of thousands of Leningraders."

Bruni had heard this deflection many times from the blockade apologists in the communist SED party. Just because the Nazis had done a bad thing didn't excuse the Soviets' doing the same horrible deed. "But wasn't that during the war, and now we have peace?" She cast her brightest smile at Vladimir, even though she doubted she'd get any valuable information out of him. That man was too well-versed in toeing the party line.

"The Soviet Union is the most peace-loving country in the world, but it's been pushed between a rock and a hard place by the constant aggression from the Americans. Or do you believe that Soviet military trucks can simply cross the Western zones without being subjected to rigorous inspections?"

"Of course not. That means, if I agree to having my papers and my suitcase inspected by the Soviet authorities, I'm free to travel to the Western zones?" She could see how the wheels in his head were moving.

"In theory you could, but unfortunately the war-mongering Western Allies have put severe restrictions on the German population and don't allow them to travel through the Soviet occupied zone."

This answer was complete bollocks, because the only ones manning the checkpoints on all streets leaving Berlin were the Soviets, and they only let people residing in East Berlin or their zone pass. In any case, Bruni decided not to press on and turned the conversation to the airlift. "So, the planes and everything is just what?"

"A delusional show of power. The American politicians are at the beck and call of the industrial magnates, who use this phony airlift to show off their new planes, hoping to gain business for air transport, thus making railways, trucks and ships obsolete."

Wow. Bruni couldn't help but give a small yelp. If this man really believed the nonsense he was spewing, he must be taking some kind of drugs. It was beyond her to fathom how any reasonable person could shun reality in such a bold way. "Thank you, I had never thought about it this way."

He seemed to be mollified by her answer and added, "Look. To call it a blockade or siege, an area must be hermetically cordoned off. As was the case with Leningrad. Berlin is an open city and it's common knowledge that the Soviet Union has offered to provide all of Berlin with coal, food, medicine and whatever else the population might need during the time that the traffic difficulties continue.

"They have even piled up loaves of bread at the Friedrichstrasse station, where every Berliner residing in the Western sectors can – and should – take what he needs. Furthermore, there's still unrestricted access to all four sectors of the city for all Berliners."

"I see. Thank you so much for your advice." Bruni had passed quite a few times through the Friedrichstrasse station, but had never seen a single breadcrumb lying around. This must be another delusional fantasy the Russian oppressors hoped would become truth if only they repeated it often enough.

"Remember, there's no blockade and if you want to evade the food shortages in the Western sectors caused by power-hungry unscrupulous American, British and French administrations, you are welcome to register at any registry office in East Berlin and the Soviets will issue ration cards for you. In contrast to the West, the USSR provides for its citizens."

Bruni forced another smile on her lips and excused

herself to hurry behind the stage or she would have vomited right on his lap.

Backstage, Heinz was waiting for her.

"Hello, Heinz." She didn't particularly like the young man with his back-combed hair slick with brilliantine and his equally glib smile. But since he was the owner's nephew, she smiled pleasantly at him.

"Hello, Bruni. Laura and I are going on a trip to the Havel riverside tomorrow and she suggested you could come with us."

Bruni's smile almost fell from her face. She was one-hundred percent sure this wasn't a social invitation, since Heinz and she never socialized, and while his girlfriend shared the apartment with Marlene, Laura and Bruni weren't anything more than acquaintances. "I'm afraid I have to work tomorrow afternoon."

"I already talked to my uncle and he's rescheduled your performance so you don't have to come in before dinner time."

He'd known she would decline and had taken precautions already. "Since you're so eager to have me around, care to let me know the reason?"

"No special reason, except that my uncle thinks you're working too much and need to get outside into the fresh air once in a while." His ears burned in a deep enough purple to be seen in the dim candlelight and Bruni knew he was lying.

"Well, thank you. At what time?"

"How about I pick you up around noon?"

"I'll be ready," Bruni said with her sweetest smile and quickly vanished into the dressing room to change into her own clothing and remove her makeup. She needed Heinz's attention like she needed a millstone around her neck, but it wasn't wise to defy his wishes, since the plot apparently had been orchestrated by Herr Schuster personally. Since she still hadn't found a committed benefactor, she depended on her job.

Half an hour later, she walked through pitch-black streets, with only the dim lights coming from the windows in the borough on current electricity-rotation guiding her home. For emergencies she always carried a torch with her, but since batteries were incredibly expensive, she used it as little as possible.

At home she lit a candle and, minutes later, went to bed, falling into a sleep filled with dreams about a handsome guy with the most magnificent dimples. Too bad she would never see Victor again.

The next day she got up before ten a.m. and had barely finished her morning routine when someone knocked on the door.

"Morning, Bruni, are you ready? Heinz is waiting downstairs with the truck," Laura said. Since fuel was a rarity, Bruni wondered why on earth he'd use the truck when going on a leisure trip. Hadn't he better save the fuel for the delivery of much-needed supplies to the cabaret?

"Thank you, I'm all set."

She squeezed into the front seat with Heinz and Laura and despite her initial aversion to going on this trip, she quite enjoyed herself as the truck rattled down the dilapidated streets southward to where the Havel broadened into a lake.

Bruni tore her eyes wide open when she saw they were headed for the British Gatow airport. In the sky, plane after plane hung like a string of pearls, landing at three-minute intervals.

Like all things military Gatow was a restricted area and Bruni caught her breath, hoping Heinz wouldn't do something stupid. But he turned toward the river and used a dirt road along the riverside until he reached a spot that was partly hidden by trees, where a small rowboat lay.

"You're not planning to make me step into that thing?" Bruni said.

Heinz chuckled. "I wouldn't dare to. No, we'll have a picnic here."

Laura unpacked a rather threadbare blanket, a water bottle, and a slice of bread and butter for each one of them. While they were eating and chatting, two skinny boys not older than ten approached and hopped into the rowboat. Heinz walked over to talk with them.

Bruni decided to enjoy the unexpected day off and lay back in the shadow of a tree. As the sun warmed her skin, she said to Laura, "This was a good idea. Thank you for inviting me."

"Out here it's easy to forget how terrible things are," Laura agreed. She tapped Bruni on the leg and both women watched as Heinz returned across the grass toward them.

"Heinz seems to be in good spirits today," Bruni commented.

"Yes. He's been in such a foul mood lately, because the blockade is bad for business."

Bruni didn't answer. Everyone suffered from the Soviets' latest action, but maybe Heinz was the one who could complain least. The cabaret was still working, thanks to his uncle's stellar connections with the American and British administrations and their need for a diversion for their soldiers.

"Wanna see something special?" Heinz asked. "There's a plane getting ready to land on the water."

Bruni turned her head and watched open-mouthed as a brilliant white plane with immense skids beneath its body glided down to smoothly land on the surface of the river.

"That was so effortless."

"It's a British Sunderland plane, specially designed to land on sea water," Heinz explained.

"Do they come all the way from England?" Bruni asked, still watching the beautiful plane glide so effortlessly across the water.

"No, that would be too far. They're coming from the Hamburg harbor."

"It's actually a great idea, since the two airports are running at capacity," Laura said.

Just then several rowboats tied up to the plane and workers began unloading the cargo. Among them Bruni recognized the two youngsters who'd mounted the rowboat minutes ago.

"Yes, but that's not the reason why they're sending them in. Salt corrodes metal, making it unsafe to be transported via plane. Not this bird though, because the Sunderlands were specifically designed to take off and land on sea water," Heinz said.

"It's brilliant." Laura patted the space beside her and Heinz flopped down and kissed her on the lips.

Bruni was still in awe over the creativity of airplane engineers and the striking beauty of this elegant bird that could land on water. She'd have to tell Victor about it...she shook her head. He wasn't here and she'd never see him again, so why did she waste her time thinking about him?

It took less than twenty minutes until the flying boat was completely unloaded, the rowboats made way to the shore and the white beauty took off into the sky. Heinz and Laura were engaged in heavy kissing and Bruni turned her head in the other direction, watching how the small boat with the two youngsters separated from the group of other boats and turned toward her location.

She suddenly had a suspicion what this leisure trip was all about. And it turned out to be correct. As soon as the youngsters landed, Heinz jumped up and walked toward them. Money exchanged hands and Heinz returned with a package. Bruni didn't ask for explanations but she assumed it was salt that the youngsters had pilfered during the hectic unloading.

19

VICTOR

The airlift was entering its second month when Victor was called to his commanding officer. He rolled up the blueprints he was working on, stuffing them back into their cardboard tube. A glimmer of hope filled his chest as he considered that maybe this time he was being called to sign his demobilization paperwork and not for another stupid and petty assignment. He'd become fed up with the Rhein-Mud airport, his asshole CO, and the utter poverty all around him, and longed to returned stateside.

"Sir." Victor entered and much to his surprise, found along with his CO Colonel Dassel an unknown general sitting at the small conference table. He saluted and stood at attention.

"Sergeant Richards?" the general asked.

"Yes, sir. That's me."

"Please sit. I'm General Tunner."

William Tunner? The man who was famous for orchestrating "the Hump", the biggest airlift operation in history.

For three years, the operation had successfully supplied Chiang Kai-shek and the US Air Force in China in their fight against the Japanese. What could this legend possibly want from him?

"Yes, sir." He took a seat across from the man who was famous across the entire Air Force but whom he'd never seen in person before. Tunner was in his early forties, rather wiry, with dark, combed-back hair and brooding eyes. He was by no means handsome, but he emanated an impressive presence. The intense stare from his eyes kept Victor alert, and for some reason he wanted to please this man.

"I assume you know why I'm here?" Tunner said.

"For the Berlin thing, sir?"

"That's how they call it here?" Tunner seemed not to be pleased and Victor made a mental note to be more careful with his words.

"As of today, I'm responsible for Operation Vittles," Tunner said. "I hear you're quite the skilled airport designer."

Victor noticed how his CO made a dour face, but obviously couldn't contradict Tunner.

"Sir, airport design and logistics is my specialty," Victor said with some pride, albeit trying to avoid self-praise.

"How would you like to build an airport from scratch?"

"I'd love to," Richard answered, even before the enormity of the question seeped into his brain.

"Great." Colonel Dassel turned to look at Victor. "As of now you've been transferred to General Tunner's command. Your new task will be the construction of a new airport in Berlin. Dismissed."

It was clear that Dassel hated Victor even more now for

being given such an opportunity, while Dassel himself was confined to office work in Frankfurt.

With a million questions in his mind, Victor glanced at his new superior, who nodded with understanding and said, "I'll see you in the operations room in thirty minutes for a briefing."

"Yes, sir, and thank you!" Victor left the office, his mind buzzing. He wasn't sure exactly what had just occurred and he knew even less whether he liked it or not. Constructing an airport from scratch had been the dream of his youth, but doing so in the rubble heap they called Berlin? While the city was blockaded by the Soviets? How could that even work? The more he thought about it, the more it seemed impossible. He'd need all kinds of raw material and heavy machinery, like bulldozers, and he wasn't sure whether any of that was available in Berlin.

Then a cold shudder ran down his spine. How would he be able to get into the besieged city? The Soviets weren't likely to lift the blockade for the man designated to build an additional airport intended to defeat their vicious action. Victor closed his eyes and put a hand on the wall next to him. Just thinking about the obvious made his knees go weak.

No way would he step into an airplane. He'd tell General Tunner that unfortunately he couldn't accept the offer for the new position. Except that his transfer hadn't been an offer.

Maybe if he became sick with a stomach flu? Or...he gave a loud sigh. Short of cutting off a leg there wasn't a thing he could do to evade his fate.

He might have to ask a friend to knock him out just before the flight and carry him onboard unconscious. Yes, that was probably the best solution.

BRUNI

The alarm rang at four in the morning and tore Bruni from a deep slumber. She barely managed to open her eyes, because once again she'd returned home from the cabaret less than two hours earlier.

Her overtired body protested and her exhausted mind pleaded with her to go to sleep again. But that would mean missing the two hours of electricity her borough was granted.

With the blockade going into its second month, living under duress had become normalcy. The Americans and British kept shuttling food and coal into Berlin and, with the little means available, kept up a minimal power service.

Bruni had never given much thought to household chores before, but now she, like every other housewife in Berlin, adjusted her schedule and slept around the times when power was available.

Leaden with tiredness, she struggled out of bed and shuffled with squinted eyes into the kitchen. There she boiled water on an electric stove, to cook potatoes and do laundry.

She didn't bother heating water for a warm bath, because she was simply too tired. A quick wash with cold water would have to do in the morning. After going about her chores, she left the potatoes in the slow cooker and the laundry to soak, before she fell back into bed. Despite her exhaustion she didn't fall asleep right away, because too many sorrows whirled in her head.

Living in Berlin under siege was the pits, and she honestly considered the idea of leaving her beloved city, because things were only going to get worse. The block-headed Russians wouldn't give an inch and everyone knew they were laughing up their sleeves and waiting for winter to come.

But the only way out was to register in their sector and that was out of the question. Again, she thought about Zara, slightly envious that her friend had left this hellhole just in time before everything went to the dogs. From thoughts about Zara her mind wandered the short distance from Wiesbaden to Frankfurt and to Victor.

It was the strangest thing, but she actually missed him. How or why, she couldn't explain. He was quite the hand-some man – and adept in bed – but entirely unsuitable. With a shudder she remembered the times her father had abused her, always pretending she was his little beloved darling. She had loved him too, until one day she hadn't. Back then Bruni had vowed never to become attached to a man again, and definitely not in the stupid emotional way she pined for Victor.

Four hours later, even though it felt like four minutes,

someone knocked on the door. Bruni turned around and placed the pillow over her head, determined to ignore whoever had come to visit. But the knocking continued, more insistent this time.

"Bruni, get up, we know you're there," a male voice shouted.

"Oh no," Bruni groaned in desperation and then yelled back, "Coming."

She put on a morning robe and dragged herself across the small apartment to open the door. Laura and Heinz were standing outside, looking excited, fresh and well-rested.

"Whatever happened to you?" Laura asked and Bruni gave a quick side-glance to the spotty mirror next to the door.

"Laundry at four in the morning."

"My mother cooked at midnight," Heinz said, swinging a metal lunch bucket.

Bruni growled something unintelligible at him. Good for him letting his mother do the work, so he didn't have to lose sleep at night. Making an effort to be polite she said, "Come in and sit down, I'll be ready in five minutes."

As much as she wished to get some more shut-eye, going with Heinz and Laura to the black market at Potsdamer Platz was more important. She still had a stash of cigarettes and hoped to barter a few things that she couldn't buy on ration cards. Having Heinz by her side would prove beneficial when it came to haggling, since he was a master negotiator and everyone at the market knew him.

They took the underground, which was running on a thinned-out schedule, to Potsdamer Platz. The location was the perfect spot for the black market, because it was located at the border triangle of the Soviet, American and British sectors. The market itself was on British ground, because the Brits had proven to be the most lenient toward black marketeers.

Nevertheless, sometimes they kept up pretenses and raided the market, although important merchants always knew in advance when this would happen and kept their most valuable merchandise away during those days. The Brits arrested a few people, let them go the next day, and everyone was happy.

Bruni had been to the market before, alone or with Marlene, but now the experience was entirely different. Stuff from beneath the counter made an appearance and a few hours later, all three of them were laden with valuable paintings, jewelry and silverware that Hans had bought. In exchange for her help, he'd paid Bruni with brand new nylon stockings, a pound of coffee and a kilo of sugar.

As far as she was concerned that was enough to turn a blind eye and not ask what he was going to do with the stuff he bought.

On their way home, they stopped at Laura's place, where her roommates Lotte and Marlene were studying for exams with another girl called Patty.

"Bruni, what a surprise! How are you?" Marlene asked as she came over to hug her friend.

"I could be better if I actually got some sleep and didn't have to get up in the middle of the night to do laundry."

"Poor you." Marlene laughed. "Do you want tea?"

"I'd love to. My throat is dry as dust after walking for hours through Potsdamer Platz."

"You've been at the black market?" Patty said, raising her eyebrow in disapproval.

Bruni thought the girl was overly prissy just because her boyfriend was a policeman. She almost giggled at the thought of what Patty and Karl would say about Heinz's purchases, but she wisely kept her mouth shut.

"Have you seen the Russian troops?" Patty asked.

"Not any more than usual." Bruni flopped down on the sofa, rubbing her feet. While walking on high heels all day probably wasn't the wisest decision, she wouldn't be caught dead in sturdy and practical shoes. Just as she'd never wear one of those horrible aprons, or worse, dungarees like many women did nowadays.

"It's just that Karl's saying the Soviets are concentrating combat troops around the perimeter of Berlin. Mongolian troops..."

Fear gripped Bruni's heart. She was probably the only woman in Berlin who hadn't been raped by the Red Army three years ago when they had *liberated* the city, thanks to her strategic alliance with Captain Feodor Orlovski. But Feodor had vanished and if the Soviets unleashed the Mongolian soldiers again on German womanhood, the only thing standing between them and another mass rape were the Americans. And while everyone hoped they'd stay in Berlin, nobody could be sure.

Maybe she should have flirted with Vladimir Rublev instead of probing him for information. He had the reputation of treating his women well and certainly had the authority to keep lowly soldiers away from her.

"Are you sure?" Marlene asked, the fear visible in her eyes.

Bruni looked around the small group; even Heinz seemed to be worried. No one wanted to relive the early days after the war when the Red Army had unleashed a horror on the Berliners that caused even the constant bombings to pale in comparison.

"Well, so far they're keeping out of Berlin, but according to Karl's boss, even Kommandant Harris is alarmed."

"Let's hope it will stay at that," Bruni said with a confidence she didn't feel. If the American Kommandant was worried, then the situation must be truly bad.

"There's nothing we can do anyways," Marlene said, fatalistic as always. "Besides, Harris announced just last night on RIAS that the Americans are not leaving Berlin. His exact words were, 'We are going to stay. I don't know the answer to the present problem—not yet—but this much I do know. The American people will not stand by and allow the German people to starve.' Then he continued with an aside to the Russians telling them they'd better be prepared if they plan on coming into the American sector."

Harris's words were meant to reassure, but Bruni still felt jumpy and wished for a white knight in shining armor to career up to her, heave her onto his horse – she actually preferred a jeep – and take her far, far away from Berlin, the blockade, and the looming Mongolian troops.

21

VICTOR

Friday, August 13, 1948

The rain pelted down on Frankfurt. Victor was looking out of the window of the flight office and noticed with trepidation the lake forming where a runway should be. He gazed up at the sky, willing the low-hanging gray clouds to clear away.

Teams of drenched and miserable German workers were getting the Skymaster planes, lined up like a string of beautiful white pearls, ready for flight. Equally drenched airmen boarded their crafts, waiting for the next scheduled bloc, when they'd all take off at ninety-second intervals.

Victor had the misfortune to be scheduled to board one of the planes together with his new CO General Tunner. The door opened and in came Tunner with a pilot, presumably the one who'd fly them to Berlin. Victor barely suppressed a gasp when he recognized the reckless young-ster Glenn Davidson.

Of all the pilots working on the supply run, it had to be him! In this instant Victor was sure that he would not survive this day.

"Richards, this is Captain Davidson, he'll run us up to Berlin."

"Yes, sir. Is it even possible to fly in this weather?" Victor couldn't resist asking the question.

Glenn broke out in a huge grin. "Sure is. We will be number twelve in the bloc. Better get going."

Tunner nodded and turned to leave the flight office with Glenn by his side. Victor had no choice but to follow them despite his protesting stomach. Never would this descent into hell come to a good end. But both Tunner and Glenn seemed to be unfazed by the awful weather conditions and engaged in a conversation about the pros and cons of flying in blocs.

Just before boarding the plane, Tunner said, "Tell Tempelhof air control that I want to try out ground controlled approach."

Victor's limbs were shaking violently. Ground controlled approach was still in an experimental stage and had not been fully developed. He studied the wicked down-pour outside and wished he had never joined the Air Force.

"It's a perfect day for such a test, sir," Glenn said. Apparently, the man didn't value his own life.

At least they didn't have to walk to the plane and get drenched like everyone else. Victor hopped into the waiting car, still somehow hoping that the whole action would be called off and he could delay having to fly for another day.

Once inside the plane, Victor sat down on the jump seat, clinging to the hope that he might be able to disembark in one piece. Right there and then he vowed to stay in Berlin until the blockade was over and he could use a train to return to his base.

The aircraft taxied to the inundated runway, taking its place in the line of birds waiting to take off. Glenn's warning to his passengers to buckle in, because it was going to be a rough flight, did nothing to instill confidence in Victor. Through the porthole he saw nothing but heavy rain, and he heard how Glenn cursed when the tower told him intervals between take-offs were getting longer and he had to wait.

Finally, the wait ended, when the co-pilot pushed the throttles forward and the powerful engines came alive. Victor was pressed back, clutching his seat, his eyes firmly closed. The roaring noise of the engines deafened him and the big aircraft shuddered like a freezing child, but suddenly the shudder smoothed out and, almost imperceptibly, the Skymaster raised its nose and took off into the skies. A smell of raw fuel wafted through the cabin. After a violent bout of queasiness, his stomach adapted to the smell, and Victor thought flying was not all that bad and maybe there was a chance for a happy end to this folly, after all.

His thoughts wandered off to the mesmerizing singer and his stomach did another somersault. He didn't expect her to pine for him, or even to remember him, but he surely had thought about her all the time. In any case it was better to imagine kissing her sweet face than conjuring up images of either crashing or having to bail out.

About ten minutes into the air, the plane bucked

violently in some turbulence. Cold sweat ran down Victor's back and the knuckles of his clasped hands became white as snow. When the aircraft was tossed about like a leaf in the autumn breeze, Victor squeezed his eyes shut, secretly hoping to die, fast and painless.

He'd rather be under gunfire from an entire Wehrmacht unit than stay one second longer in this death machine. Desperately trying to occupy his mind with anything but the imminent crash, he recalled memories of the night he spent with Bruni, making love to her. The softness of her skin, her eager reaction to his caresses...

"We've reached the corridor through the Soviet zone," Glenn said into the intercom. "The ride might get jumpy, because I can't circumvent bad weather zones."

Might get jumpy? And what has it been until now? Panic struck Victor's system and he fought the urge to draw his weapon and force Glenn to make an emergency landing.

While Glenn forcefully clasped his hands around the yoke of the rolling, bumping, tossing and bucking Skymaster to keep them inside the twenty-mile-wide corridor, Victor did the same with the seating surface of the jump seat. He did not want to imagine what would happen should they be blown out of the corridor...would the Soviets dare to shoot them down?

Just then it occurred to him that he didn't have a parachute, and even if he did, he wouldn't know what to do with it. In a last effort to remain calm he stared at General Tunner's back. If the general placed his confidence in Glenn's flying expertise, so would he. That and advanced technology. Victor sent a short prayer to heaven that his engineering colleagues had done a stellar job on the brand-new radarscopes in Berlin. These wonders of the modern world could see where the human eye couldn't and were able to pick up aircraft even through clouds and rain, guiding them safely to their landing point.

But his prayers weren't heard. Excited voices came from the intercom. Apparently two planes departing from Gatow to return home in the central corridor had lost their way and drifted into the southern corridor with the incoming planes of Victor's bloc.

"Zero visibility," Glenn said into his headset and, after orders from the control tower, took the aircraft higher.

After several minutes Glenn at the yoke and General Tunner looking over his shoulder visibly relaxed, and Victor asked, "What happened?"

"Ground controlled approach talked down the first three Big Easy planes coming from Frankfurt without a problem. Now we just have to wait for our turn," Glenn said.

But then the tension in the cockpit became thick and almost instantly, it felt as if the old Skymaster was shooting straight up into the air. Victor glimpsed at the altitude meter. It crept impossibly high, leaving the 10,000 feet mark behind. Panic pressed the air from Victor's lungs, because this couldn't be a good thing.

The flight engineer turned around and explained, "Big Easy four missed his approach and has to go around, therefore we have to fly waiting circles in the holding pattern along with the remaining planes in our bloc."

Victor's dizziness became stronger and he tried to breathe against the feeling of having to vomit. He focused his attention on looking out of the front window, but there was nothing to see except for a thick gray soup. He feared that any moment another aircraft would appear out of the nothing and they'd inevitably crash into it.

Apparently a veritable traffic jam had arisen from the missed approach of Big Easy four. Despite his own distress, he realized that General Tunner was about to explode with anger. They were flying ever-higher circles over Berlin and the cockpit was filled with constant chatter from the radio.

"Big Easy four is on his second approach," Glenn said and everyone in the aircraft held their breath anxiously awaiting the news of a safe landing.

It didn't come.

"Damn!" Glenn shouted loud enough to be heard over the noise of the engine and the flight engineer again turned around, handing Victor an oxygen mask, while Glenn announced through the intercom. "We have to go higher. Big Easy four crashed and the airfield is littered with wreckage. No landings possible."

The sick feeling returned. Victor pressed the oxygen mask over his face and caught a glimpse of the altitude meter. Fifteen thousand feet.

Was this the day the airlift ended for good? The Soviets seemed to have made a pact with the weather and were surely laughing their asses off at the helpless American aircraft struggling with squalls and clouds.

By now Victor had completely forgotten about his own fear, and just prayed that all the crews would be able to land safely. Even someone as inexperienced as he was with flying knew that they were in imminent danger.

"Sir, we need to get them all down now or..." Glenn said.

"Or what?" General Tunner responded.

"Or this will become a downright mess. The next bloc of

thirty planes coming from Wiesbaden will be here in less than five minutes and then a mid-air collision is almost guaranteed."

Tunner didn't answer, but about ten seconds later he picked up the microphone and spoke with a calm but loud voice. "This is General Tunner to control tower. Send all Big Easy aircraft except for Big Easy twelve back to their base. I repeat, every single Big Easy over Berlin or in the corridor is to return home. No craft is to take off until I give new orders."

Victor couldn't hear what the tower said, but moments later Tunner spoke again, "Return all Big Easy aircraft to their base. Then tell me when it's safe to land."

Ten minutes later Victor left the airplane with wobbly knees, incredibly grateful that the general had kept his cool and defused a possibly catastrophic situation.

22

VLADI

Vladi had spent most of the day at the Berlin Air Safety Center, one of the two four-power institutions still in operation. He had witnessed the crash, the emergency landing, and most importantly the return home with their tails between their legs of the remaining aircraft.

It had been an unexpectedly successful day.

With a smile on his face he left the Air Safety Center and jumped into his jeep to bring General Sokolov the good news. The old man was getting increasingly malicious, since all the news so far had been good news for their enemy. But today the Americans and British had sucked up their first major defeat, and Vladi would be the message-bearer.

"Comrade General. I bring good tidings." Vladi entered Sokolov's office in Karlshorst to find a very grumpy man, who was obviously plagued by his ulcers again.

"Comrade Rublev. Sit down and tell me."

Vladi took a seat on the chair in front of the huge oak desk. "I've been at the Air Safety Center—"

"I don't want to hear anything about this bloody flying circus!"

"Comrade General, the flying circus was sent home today." Now he had Sokolov's attention. "In fact, there were at least two major accidents and an emergency landing. The much-hyped ground controlled approach didn't work out as planned and in the end all the aircraft but one were sent home."

Vladi preferred not to mention it was General Tunner's plane that had touched down in Tempelhof. He'd done his homework and read everything about Tunner's fame and his experience in air logistics. *The Hump* was considered the biggest and most successful air supply run in the history of mankind.

"It was about time. But are you sure they won't be back?"

That was a tricky question. Vladi didn't want to seem overconfident because he might be held to his assertion, but he had to sound positive.

"Comrade General, I believe this was not the last we have seen of them. Once the weather clears up they will continue with this ridiculous show." He could see how Sokolov's expression darkened and hurried to add, "But as soon as the weather turns bad again, and it will, they will face the same problems. Due to the climatic conditions in Germany, they probably won't be able to keep up their flights much longer than October 15."

"It's about time the Americans stop their little charade that pretends to supply the population with food when the real goal is to pillage and ransack the city. This so-called humanitarian operation is nothing but a badly disguised robbery. Blaupunkt, for example, produces five thousand radios per month and do you know what happens to them?"

Vladi knew the answer; nevertheless he indulged Sokolov and asked, "No, Comrade General, I don't. What happens to the radios?"

"They aren't sold to the Berlin population, no, they are extracted from the city and sent to the Western zones. And do you know how this is accomplished?" Sokolov's face had taken on a shade of deep purple and he was fighting for breath. "With the airlift, of course. Same thing happens to the production of Osram. The entire monthly output of two million light bulbs is disappearing into Western Germany. I ask you, what good does this so-called airlift do when all it does is to steal the entire production of Berlin companies? Goods and merchandise that belong to the Berlin population and not to the greedy big industrialists. In fact, our goal must be to stop the bleeding out of production capital into the hands of the rich and scheming imperialists. That is the true humanitarian mission." The door opened and Sokolov's secretary stepped in, but he didn't deign to look at her or interrupt his monologue.

"At the Gatow airport the British thieves have installed a special intermediary who buys valuable tools and instruments, paying in illegally printed Deutsche "B" Mark, loading them into the cargo planes, and once in Western Germany he sells the goods for a handsome profit. Merchandise that belongs to the Berliners, who have produced them at a great sacrifice using their last natural resources. Does this sound like a humanitarian operation to you?"

"No, Comrade General, it doesn't." Vladi wondered how

Sokolov knew about the intermediary in Gatow, since that airport was highest security clearance and not even Red Army Intelligence had been able to plant a spy there. Due to Gatow's location away from the city center it was even more reclusive and better secured from Soviet spying than the American Tempelhof airport.

"There is no need for an air bridge except for the need of the American and British mobs to pilfer, rob and sequester everything that is worth a single *Pfennig*! This has to end. Now!" The general jumped from his seat and agitatedly paced the room. "We need to implement emergency measures."

In this moment Sokolov seemed to become aware of his secretary and shouted at her, "Go. Get me Colonel Ulyanin. Now!"

She scurried off like a frightened mouse and Vladi felt sympathy for her. It wasn't easy to work for someone like Sokolov.

"You can leave, Comrade Rublev."

As much as Vladi would have liked to be privy to what kind of measures the general had in mind, he had no business to ask or wait around until the air forces commander, Ulyanin, arrived. They wouldn't dare to shoot down the American and British planes. Or would they?

23

VICTOR

Despite the pelting rain, Victor left his new quarters at the American garrison and walked to the waiting jeep. He'd asked a driver to bring him to the French sector, where he had a meeting with the head of engineering, Captain Pierre Lejeune.

Tegel, the chosen location for the new airport, was a former military training area that had been flattened during the war.

"Sorry. I'm not late, am I?" he asked the driver.

"No, sir. I was just a few minutes early."

"Good." Victor sat back and watched the city streets pass them by as the vehicle headed north, when he suddenly recognized the street that led to the Café de Paris. A smile appeared on his lips as he remembered his night with Bruni. Maybe he'd have the time to visit the cabaret tonight. It would be a nice closure to an otherwise awful day.

The driver stopped the jeep on an open field, although mud pool would have been a more appropriate description.

"Something wrong?" Victor asked.

"No, sir, we've arrived."

"Arrived where?"

"Didn't you say you wanted to go to Tegel? This is it."

Victor could barely believe his eyes, but he saw the man wasn't joking. The driver pointed with his thumb to a trailer halfway across the muddy field. "That's construction command center. Sorry, but I can't drive there in this mud."

Victor closed his greatcoat and gave a sorrowful look at his freshly polished boots. But there was no way around it; he had to brave the elements on foot. A thought occurred to him.

"Do they have telephone or radio in that shack?"

The driver laughed good-naturedly. "They sure do. Although it's only in French."

Very funny. Victor bypassed the worst deluges, but he still waded ankle deep in sludge, his boots making squishing sounds as he trudged forward. In less than a minute he was completely drenched, raindrops running down his neck and soaking his shirt beneath the greatcoat.

A single crawler tractor was idling at the side of the future airfield. For the thousandth time on this day he questioned his own sanity and cursed the fact that he hadn't stayed in the States, working at an airport dispatching war birds to Europe and the Pacific. It would have been a nice safe post to sit out the war in.

But no, he'd volunteered *to go where the action was.* And now he was fighting his way across a slimy pool of mud, about to discuss how to build an airport on this devastated piece of land – with a Frenchman, no less – with virtually no machinery, no raw materials and no skilled labor.

What a great plan.

He opened the door of the construction trailer and a gust of wind pushed it from his hand, slamming it against the trailer's wall.

"*Hé! Ferme la porte, imbécile. Ça mouille!*" someone shouted.

"I'm sorry." Victor grabbed the door and closed it, before he peeked into the trailer, which looked refreshingly dry and clean. A man in his fifties with sparse dark hair and a beaked nose sat at a small desk filled with piles of maps, papers, pencils, liners and more. Victor involuntarily shivered at the disorganization. "Are you Captain Lejeune?"

"Yes, and you must be Sergeant Richards? I'm Pierre, by the way."

Victor sighed with relief when he realized Lejeune's English was surprisingly good if heavily accented, and he didn't have to dig out his own miserable school French. "Yes, I'm here to oversee the construction of the airport."

"Glad you're finally here, I can really use some help. First of all, we need…" Lejeune rattled off a list of dozens of items needed for the building site, none of them currently available in Berlin.

"Wait!" Victor interrupted. "I'd like to get the big picture first."

Several hours later Victor had his work cut out for him, and he was just about to leave when Pierre said, "So whatever you need, you let me know and I will see about getting approval for it."

Victor chose his next words carefully. "I thought the Americans are building this thing?"

"*Mais oui*. But Tegel is in our sector, so everything has to be approved by General Ganeval."

This was news to Victor, and he planned on having a word about this with General Tunner, since he had no intention of getting caught up in having to wait for French approval on all the steps, but Pierre's next words sweetened the deal.

"You may not have noticed because of the bad weather, but we have hired some workers already, and can get more anytime. We just need you to say how many."

Not having to worry about labor would take a huge load off his shoulders. He already had an impossible task at hand with finding the raw materials and the heavy machinery. Still, he wasn't entirely convinced. "What kind of workers?"

"Mostly unskilled labor. For lack of machinery they've been doing everything manually. Sweeping mines, clearing up debris and levelling the ground."

Victor couldn't imagine that some people could replace the heavy machinery usually used and move such an immense project forward. Especially not in the required timeframe. General Clay had voiced his wish to have the Tegel airport ready well before winter. That left Victor with three months, four at most. "Exactly how many people have you hired?"

"About a thousand." Pierre seemed completely unfazed by the staggering number.

"One thousand?"

"Yes, and that's only the beginning. We plan to ramp up our workforce to ten thousand within the week."

Where on earth did the Frenchman hope to get that many people on such short notice? Pierre seemed to have read his mind, because he said, "You wouldn't know what people here are willing to do for extra rations. We pay them good money, but what they covet most is the hot meal we give them as well."

Victor could only shake his head. It was hard to believe Pierre's outrageous claim. Berliners worked for food?

Pierre raised his voice again. "You don't have to concern yourself with any of this. You just tell me where to put the workers and I'll organize the rest. We have planned rotating shifts twenty-four hours around the clock, seven days a week."

"Sounds good." Maybe this airport was feasible after all. Victor didn't have any of the construction material he normally required, but it seemed he'd have an army of willing workers to replace everything else.

Pierre glanced at his watch. "I'm sorry but I need to leave for a briefing. Tomorrow I'll introduce you to the engineers and foremen and as soon as the storm subsides, we can resume work.

"I'll see you in the morning, then."

"Do you want me to give you a ride to the American garrison?"

"That would be perfect. Thanks."

Content with the results of his meeting, Victor took up residence in his quarters. After a hot shower and an evening meal, he was too exhausted to consider anything else but getting some shut-eye.

Visiting Bruni would have to wait another day. He'd stay here for at least three months, and it wasn't as if she could leave the city and disappear.

24

BRUNI

Bruni and Marlene disembarked the underground train, along with hundreds of other Berliners. They were headed to Platz der Republik, where the Lord Mayor Ernst Reuter would be addressing the people in front of the burned-out Reichstag.

"Do you know who's here?" Marlene said as they weaved through the multitude of people, hoping to find their friends at the agreed-upon meeting point.

"All of Berlin, it seems." Bruni pursed her lips, giving a muttered curse when someone bumped into her.

"No, I mean not here, but in the city."

"Do you expect me to guess?" Bruni was getting annoyed. It hadn't been her idea to come to this public concourse; if she'd had her say, she'd now be sitting in her apartment, drinking wine from the black market and listening to the speech on the radio.

But no, Lotte and Marlene had insisted they go and witness this *historic moment* in person. Where was Lotte anyway? She was quite tall and her flaming red hair should be seen from far away.

"I thought it would be fun, but you'll never guess anyway."

"Guess what?"

Marlene glared at Bruni. "Are you even listening to me?"

"Not really. I've been looking for Lotte and the others." Bruni hated people who were late.

"Maybe they got held up somewhere." Marlene's eyes twinkled with mischief. "Victor is in Berlin."

Bruni's breath left her lungs and a strange emotion zipped through her body, but she barely raised her left eyebrow and said coolly, "Oh. You mean that American soldier from Frankfurt? What's he doing here?"

"Oh, Bruni, you can't fool me. Ever since you and he disappeared so quickly after Zara's farewell party, you've been different. Haven't even gushed about another guy."

"That's not true." Bruni said, even though it was. For whatever reason, she hadn't been able to get Victor out of her mind. Now that he was in Berlin…her heart did a double take…but then her elation deflated. Why hadn't he come to see her? It could only mean he wasn't interested. And she most certainly wouldn't throw herself at a man. *An unsuitable one*, she reminded herself. "Where did you even see him?"

"He came to the university."

"What?" Bruni was about to launch into a thorough interrogation when someone waved at them and shouted. "Bruni! Marlene! Over here!"

Of course, Lotte and Patty had chosen this very moment to arrive. Bruni glared at Marlene, even while she waved back and said, "You will tell me every last detail later."

"And here I thought you weren't interested in him." Marlene giggled. Seconds later, they hugged their friends.

"What about Laura and Heinz? Haven't they arrived yet?" Patty asked.

"No. But it's awfully difficult to find anyone in this crowd. And where's Karl?" Marlene asked.

"Up there beside the stage, working." Patty scrunched up her nose. Having a policeman as boyfriend meant that he usually had to work when everyone else was out to have fun. While some might feel sorry for her because of that, Bruni saw the positives. Karl had a secure job and was paid well. He had good connections to the Allies and could often arrange things that other people couldn't. It was the next best thing to having an Allied soldier for a boyfriend.

"I never expected this many people to turn out," Bruni said.

Lotte laughed. "That's because you're always holed up in the cabaret by night and sleeping during the day. Have you even noticed there's a blockade going on?"

"Very funny." Bruni made a sulky face. "I'm not that out of touch. Honestly, as much as I love Berlin, I won't stay here if the communists take over."

"By the way, have you heard from Zara?" It was Patty who asked the question.

"Nothing. We're worried sick about her."

A harrumphing from the podium caught their attention, along with the estimated three hundred thousand other attendees, and a silence fell over the place. Everyone wanted to listen to the Lord Mayor's speech.

Ernst Reuter was sixty years old, completely gray with a far-receding hairline and piercing eyes. He was a wiry man, easily underestimated, but when he talked, people listened in awe. Ever since he'd returned from Turkey, where he'd spent the war years in exile, after being released from a concentration camp in 1935, he had been a beacon of hope for the Berliners.

His standing among the population and his conviction to fight for freedom was so powerful that the Soviets had vetoed his election to Lord Mayer two times in the past year.

The Lord Mayor raised his voice. "We will return! We will return into the Soviet sector of Berlin and we will return into the Soviet occupied zone in Germany.

"Today is the day when it is not diplomats and generals who talk and negotiate. Today is the day when the people of Berlin raise their voices. We, the people, call upon the world for support in our struggle for democracy.

"We want to give the communist SED party one piece of advice: if it needs a new symbol, it shouldn't be the handshake, but the handcuffs that its members were putting on the Berliners. The handcuffs are the true symbol of these pathetic weeds, who sold themselves and their people for a few Marks to a foreign power.

"When today the people of Berlin are gathered here in hundreds of thousands, we know that the world is watching. If you abandon this city and its people, you also abandon the world, and yourself.

"We've been through this once before. We've had one dictatorial party and we don't want another."

Cheers rose from the crowd in support of his words.

Reuter raised his hands again after allowing the crowds to express their feelings for a minute. When he lowered his hands, the people grew quiet once more.

"You nations of the world, you people in America, in England, in France, in Italy! Look upon this city and realize that you must not abandon Berlin and its people. There is but one possibility for all of us: to stick together until this fight ends with a victory over the power of darkness.

"The people of Berlin have spoken. We have done our duty and will continue to do it. Nations of the World! Now do your duty and help us during this time before us. Not only with the roaring of your planes, but also with your determination to stand for our mutual ideals, because that alone can guarantee our future and your future.

"Nations of the World, look upon Berlin! And Berliners, rest assured, we will win this fight!"

The crowd was frantic. They howled and cheered and chanted. Bruni glanced around and saw hope and determination in every face. Right now, there was no doubt, they'd come out on the other side. The Russian Bear had tried to squish them in his paw, but they'd hopped down and together with the Western Allies, who were fast becoming friends instead of occupiers, the Berliners would chase away the bear and live in peace and freedom once more.

Even Bruni, who'd never considered herself a political person, felt a sense of pride. She fell into the chanting with the others in the crowd. This was the future. Perhaps she wouldn't be forced to leave her beloved Berlin, because however much she whined and complained, it was her home and she'd leave it with a heavy heart.

Overwhelmed with emotions, she didn't pay attention to what was going on around her.

"Look at this!" Marlene nudged her arm and pointed to the Brandenburg Gate to her right. Once a proud symbol, it was now riddled with bullet holes, and the elegant Quadriga that had graced the monument had been destroyed. The monument itself had somehow survived the war, and now marked the border between the British and Soviet sectors.

During Hitler's reign, the Nazis had taken great delight in hanging a large swastika from the top. Now, the Russians had followed suit, flying an oversized red flag. Several youths had become riled up during the speech and were now scaling the Brandenburg Gate in an attempt to reach the top.

Bruni tapped Laura on the shoulder and soon everyone around them was watching the three boys on their climb. At first Bruni had no idea what they were after.

She and her friends weren't the only ones who watched the youngsters Argus-eyed. A group of Russians soldiers marched toward gate, yelling and waving. When they brandished their rifles, the gathered crowd paused and waited with bated breath for whatever would happen next.

Bruni thought the Russians wouldn't be stupid enough to shoot three boys in cold blood, and in front of three hundred thousand eyewitnesses, plus television cameras.

Meanwhile the boys reached the top of the monument and tore down the symbol of despised oppressors. They crumpled up the Soviet flag and waved it in the air like a trophy, much to the delight of the crowd of onlookers.

Then they began their descent, glowing with delight. By the time they had reached the ground, intending to make a beeline for the safety of the British sector only about twenty yards away, the Russians had caught up with them.

A murmur went through the crowd and Bruni held her breath, hoping for the best. Just when the Russians were about to grab the three youngsters, salvation appeared in the form of a British provost marshal. He illegally crossed the border into the Russian sector and used his swagger stick to push the soldiers away from the Germans. The three boys didn't waver and quickly dashed behind the borderline.

"Oh my God, that was close!" Bruni yelped.

"Stupid boys, they could have died." Lotte rolled her eyes. "The Russians are not to be trifled with. They've been known to shoot people for less." Lotte's boyfriend Johann was still a Soviet prisoner of war somewhere in Siberia, and having met many of his released comrades, she never held back her contempt for the Soviets.

She probably was right. Although Bruni personally had always been on good terms with the Russian officers who came to the cabaret, she knew that the man alone was different from the system. Even poor Feodor had fallen victim to his own government after they'd lost the elections in 1946.

But the young men weren't out of danger yet, because a jeepload of Russian soldiers arrived, jumped off the vehicle and ran after the Germans, violating the border between the sectors in the same way the British provost marshal had done mere seconds before. Bruni watched with her mouth gaping wide open. This was more exciting than the last movie she'd watched. Oblivious to the danger for herself, she pressed forward to better see.

The British were quick to react and put a squad of military police between the boys and the Russians. At this point, the crowd was so riled up, there was no going back. Some intrepid Germans surged over into the Russian side, yelling and screaming. Their shouts became louder and soon everyone chanted, "Drive the Russians back to Moscow! Drive the Communists out of Berlin!"

Bruni was fascinated. She'd never before been in such a unified crowd, and sensed how an eager agitation took possession of her. She was about to run toward the Brandenburg Gate herself, but was yanked back.

"This is getting out of hand," Marlene yelled into her ear. "We need to get out of here, fast."

Disappointment washed over Bruni, but she obliged and followed Marlene, who steered them through the throng of people across the huge plaza. They hadn't covered a lot of distance when shots rang out and Bruni's brain stopped working.

Instantaneous, the crowd transformed into a flock of headless chickens, running aimlessly in different directions. Only thanks to Marlene's merciless grip on her arm did Bruni manage to stumble forward and eventually board a train.

"My goodness, Bruni, whatever happened to you? You were about to launch yourself at one of the Russian soldiers."

"I don't know." Slowly, Bruni came into her senses again. It was as if she'd been under a magic spell, eager to run with the mob.

Marlene sighed. "It's the lure of mass gatherings. The atmosphere shifts and people don't think clearly anymore.

It is as if some common spirit takes over the individual minds. Hitler and Goebbels were masters at using this phenomenon for their purposes."

"Since when are you a psychologist?" Bruni was shaken, but didn't want Marlene to know.

"I'm not, but our criminal law teacher had us study crimes committed by mobs. It works the exact way things unfolded today. Scary."

Bruni nodded. "What about the others?"

"No idea. We lost them when you were pressing toward the Brandenburg Gate, but I gather they were wise enough to stay out of trouble. Lotte was in the same lecture about mass hysteria."

As they stepped out of the train and emerged in the American sector, they walked to Marlene's apartment, where they met the other girls.

"Thank God, you're here!" Lotte hugged them tight. "We were so worried about you."

"We got stuck in the crowd and had to fight our way to the underground, which naturally was completely over-crowded. I think we waited almost an hour for a train to board," Marlene explained and Bruni was grateful that her friend didn't mention Bruni's lapse.

"Have you heard? The Russians shot four Berliners dead." Patty was close to tears; she must be worried about her policeman boyfriend.

Several days later, a very long and impressive funeral procession took place, moving past the Platz der Republik, the Reichstag and the Brandenburg Gate. Bruni hadn't intended to participate, still shocked from her own reaction to the events on that fateful day, but Marlene convinced her it was a necessary show of solidarity with the departed. A signal to the Russians that Berliners would never be defeated, would never crumble.

The Russian bear was just that: a threat to one human, but easily scared away and defeated by a group of them.

Reluctantly Bruni joined her in the sad procession. The depth of emotion the entire city was showering upon those who'd died and those responsible for the loss of these lives was impressive. If the Russians had been disliked before, now they were hated with a passion that was hard to match.

VICTOR

Victor slammed his fist onto the desk in the construction trailer. "This simply doesn't work. We need more heavy machinery!"

"We have commandeered the only functioning crawler tractor available in the Western sectors, and two tractor units—" Pierre said in his heavy accent.

"It's not enough. I can't be expected to build an airport purely with manpower." Victor scratched his head. Manpower, or actually womanpower, was the only thing they had in abundance.

The French had quickly expanded the organization and now employed nineteen thousand Germans, half of them women, who eagerly showed up for their eight-hour-shift and ground their fingers to the bone with nothing more than a shovel to help.

He'd never imagined that even the tiniest, thinnest women would power through the hard drudgery with such seemingly inexhaustible energy. Day in, day out, they worked in three shifts on the airfield, collecting stones, digging, flattening, turning the cement mixer and so much more. But there was only a certain amount of work humans could do, no matter how enthusiastic they were.

"I need bulldozers and cranes!" Even to Victor's own ears he sounded like a petulant toddler.

"*Mais oui*, nothing easier than that – we simply ask the Russians to give them to us. Or to lift the blockade, if that would help your predicament?" Pierre had a strange sense of humor and oftentimes Victor simply stared at him in disbelief, before he noticed the smirk on Pierre's lips and deduced that the other man was joking.

On the other side of the trailer, James, one of the American engineers, was fiddling with a soldering iron, fixing whatever device had broken down. Without James' creativity they would be even more meagerly supplied.

"Pierre is right." James turned around, a cigarette hanging in the corner of his mouth. "Every single piece of equipment that survived the war has been dismantled and shipped to Russia long ago. And since nobody in the West foresaw the blockade and the need to build another airport, we didn't bring in new equipment."

Victor scowled. "On whose side are you? Apparently with the French."

James grinned and joined in the friendly banter. "I'm on the side of reason. And your whining is unreasonable. If there's no equipment here, and it's too big to fly in, then we have to make it." With these words James turned back to his soldering iron.

"He may have a point," Pierre said. "But how?"

"We can't make a crane, but…" Victor walked over to look over James's shoulder. "Supposedly you can put together anything that is in pieces?"

"Sure can. Gimme the parts and I make it whole again!" James beamed with pride. As a boy he'd probably tweaked his motor scooter to death.

Victor scratched his chin and paced the small trailer, thinking out loud, "What if…someone in Frankfurt dismantled a crane into parts small enough to fit into a Skymaster? Would you be able to put it back together?"

Both James and Pierre looked at him with wide-open eyes. "*Tu es fou*. Not only crazy, but haywire."

But James shook his head. "It might work…lemme think about it."

After a lengthy discussion they concluded they would need two gifted mechanics working closely together, one in Frankfurt and one in Berlin. James naturally considered himself to be the designated genius in Berlin.

The team in Frankfurt had to dismantle the equipment, put a number on each part, make a construction plan with the numbered parts and load the neatly packed boxes into the next Skymaster. In Berlin James would oversee a team of mechanics who welded the equipment back together according to the numbered manual.

"Easy as pie, a simple construction kit, but writ large." James beamed from ear to ear and Victor decided to present this brilliant idea to General Tunner.

Ten minutes later he had him on the phone and after some initial disbelief, the general promised to talk with the right people in Wiesbaden or Frankfurt and make it possible.

After this breakthrough, Victor told Pierre and James that he'd go for a walk to do some thinking and probably wouldn't be back before morning.

Apart from thinking through the practicalities of the new plan, Victor had something else in mind. After working sixteen hours a day for these last weeks, he wanted to use the opportunity and see Bruni tonight.

Glancing at his wristwatch he realized it was too late to catch her at her place, so he decided to visit the Café de Paris instead.

She was just finishing her song and getting ready to disappear behind the curtain when he caught her eye. His mouth turned up in greeting and hers did the same. His heart beat a little faster. She hadn't forgotten about him.

He didn't know what to expect from this meeting, didn't even know what to say, but he was incredibly happy. By the bright smile on her face, and most importantly, the twinkle in her eyes, she felt the same way. She slipped off the side of the stage and rushed toward him in a very unladylike manner.

Victor rose to his full height, and despite her high heels, he still towered over her. His hands itched to caress her beautiful face, but he didn't dare do so in the crowded place. "Hello, gorgeous. I hoped I might find you still working here."

"Took you long enough!" She pouted.

Flabbergasted he noticed the angry glint in her eyes. "Will you sit with me for a moment?"

She nodded and raised her hand to alert the waitress. "If you're going to buy me champagne."

"Is there still champagne in Berlin?" He actually didn't want an honest answer, because everyone knew that despite the Russians' official disdain for contraband, many of their soldiers lived quite nicely because of it.

"You should know best. You work for General Tunner." Bruni leaned back, near enough to make the latent attraction flare to life, but too far to actually touch.

"You're well informed."

"I've been told you've been here for two weeks already." Her voice held a distinct reproach.

"I'm sorry. I've wanted to come and see you but there never was enough time, we've been working around the clock." He put his hand on her arm. "I've missed you."

Before she could answer the waitress arrived and he ordered champagne for both of them. Together with the transfer to Berlin had come a substantial raise and a promotion to Sergeant Major.

When the champagne arrived they clinked glasses, and her wonderful blue eyes all but drove him out of his mind. Looking at her luscious red lips, he wanted nothing more than to kiss her.

Instead he took a curl that fell beneath her ear between his fingers and asked, "Let me make it up to you tonight. When you are finished here, will you let me drive you home?

"I'd love to." She moved nearer to him, leaving less than a hair's breadth between their shoulders, and he sensed her shiver. The anticipation of being alone with her became almost unbearable.

"I'll wait for you right here." Victor's voice was hoarse with desire.

She nodded, emptied her glass and then gracefully stood up. "I have one more performance. After I'm finished wait ten minutes and then pick me up at the back entrance."

His heart jumped.

26

BRUNI

Bruni woke up with a heavy arm across her breast. She wiggled out from under it and watched Victor sleeping. His dirty blond hair was tousled and more than just a shadow of stubble adorned his cheeks. He rolled over smiling but didn't open his eyes. She itched to trace his dimples with her fingers but was afraid she'd wake him up.

Fondly remembering last night, she slipped out of bed, put on a morning robe and touched up her makeup before she walked into the kitchen to raid her meager supplies and make him a hearty breakfast.

Dried milk, dried eggs and coffee was all she could offer. With a shrug she decided she was not going to bother; he'd want to eat at the garrison anyway. She made coffee on a portable gas stove and gasped, startled, when suddenly an arm snaked around her waist.

She jumped backward, straight into Victor's chest. As he turned her around and smacked a big kiss on her lips, she noticed he was completely naked, just as when they'd fallen asleep in each other's arms. Memories rushed back and she pressed her face against his hairy chest.

"Sorry, sweetheart, but I have to run or I'll be late for the meeting with my French colleague. Do you have breakfast for me?"

"Don't you go to the garrison first?" The shock must have been clearly visible on her face, because his voice was full of concern when he answered.

"No, from here to Tegel it's a stone's throw, but if I return to the garrison first I'll need an hour at least."

"I can whip up something for you, but," she nibbled on her lips, anxious what he'd say about her less than stellar cooking skills and the meager choice of ingredients, "you're probably used to better food at the garrison."

He laughed. "Then I'll have to bring my own provisions if we're going to make this a habit."

Bruni felt herself flush, which was completely out of character for her. To conceal her mixed feelings, she turned away and mixed the dried egg powder with hot water from the thermos while he left the kitchen to wash and get dressed.

When he returned, they both settled in at the kitchen table.

Victor didn't flinch, but she sensed that he found the breakfast awful. Normally that wouldn't concern her, because it was his problem, but for some reason she wanted him to like her food.

Personally, she'd more or less grown accustomed to the dirt-like taste of the dried stuff every Berliner lived on, but it was nothing to write home about.

"That was great, thank you, sweetheart," Victor said as he stood up to put his plate into the sink.

"Don't lie to me. Dried eggs are awful. Everyone knows it, but we still eat it, because it's the only food we have. Along with dried milk, dried potatoes, dried meat and fresh bread, because that's made from dry flour."

He chuckled and brushed his thumb across her cheek, an incredibly intimate gesture that filled her heart with warmth and fear at the same time. "This blockade won't last forever and then there'll be fresh food again."

"Promise?" she asked with a coy glance.

"Promise. And next time I'll bring food from the garrison for us."

Bruni's heart beat staccato. He seemed to think they were officially a pair. Naturally that was out of the question. She might be crazily attracted to him and even get butterflies in her stomach whenever she caught a glimpse of his handsome face with those cute dimples, but she reminded herself that she was on the lookout for a captain at least. Someone who could afford her the lifestyle she wanted. Someone like Dean Harris.

"About that…" she said slowly.

"You don't want to see me again?" Disappointment was thick in his voice.

"I do, but look, I'm not a girl who dreams of falling in love and marrying. This is just a casual relationship, no strings attached."

The bright light in his wonderful gray-green eyes dimmed, but he nodded. "I never talked about marriage. I just like being with you."

"And I like being with you, but I want you to understand

that you don't have dibs on me, just because we're sleeping together. A man can conquer my body, but never my heart."

That's the way she'd handled it throughout her life, because after she'd run away from home, she'd vowed never again to love a man. And it had served her well.

But with Victor, the wall around her heart was crumbling, and she didn't like that one bit. It would only lead to heartbreak for either one or both of them. The intelligent thing would be to cut off this right now and never see him again...

She couldn't bring herself to do that. Because, unlike other men she'd consorted with, she genuinely yearned to be with Victor. That hadn't happened with either Feodor or Dean. They had simply been a pleasurable way of getting what she wanted.

Bruni led Victor to the door and kissed him on the lips. "See me at the club, will you?"

"I most definitely will."

27

VICTOR

The first Skymaster arrived with neatly numbered parts on wooden pallets, and subsequent planes arrived daily for two weeks. The man who'd overseen the dismantling of the equipment also arrived in Berlin and went straight to work with James and a handful of German mechanics.

The big brass had initially opposed using Germans for such a responsible task, but there simply weren't enough Americans who could do the job. All the skilled men were needed in airplane maintenance, a field the bosses wanted to contract out even less.

Victor inspected the work a few times a day, impressed at the fast progress and confident that with the new dredger, steam roller, crane, and wheeled loader the Tegel airport would be finished by December, which was two months out. When he saw that James' team didn't need his supervision, he returned to his trailer and began fine-tuning the priorities and making sure each supervising engineer had enough manpower to handle his next task.

The bottlenecks were always the raw materials, since everything from cement, tarmac and steel to wooden poles, brick stones and paint had to be flown in by air. He constantly haggled with General Harris about how much tonnage he was assigned, because that had to be axed from the food portion of deliveries.

The phone rang and Pierre answered it. He held out the receiver and said, "Victor, *Général* Harris's secretary is asking you to move your afternoon meeting with him forward."

Victor took the receiver and told the secretary that he could be at the American headquarters in forty-five minutes. Then he asked Pierre, "Can I borrow the project driver? I'll send him back immediately."

"*Mais oui.* Better not keep the boss waiting."

Victor gathered his blueprints and the lists with supply needs, stuffed them into his briefcase and was on his way. He respected Harris a great deal. The man had a knack not only for numbers, but also for people. The Berliners loved him and it was amazing to see the cheers and jubilation whenever he drove through the streets in his open-roofed jeep.

But more importantly, Harris had made the airlift his personal task. While General Tunner was running the show, managing the logistics and tweaking the operation in the air to allow more planes to land at shorter intervals with fewer accidents, Harris took care of the supply side.

He occupied a team of mathematicians, doctors and dietary advisers in calculating, down to the last calorie, how much a person needed to subsist. It was Harris' doing that fifty tons of oranges from Florida were flown to Berlin, considered an unnecessary luxury by most everyone, but according to his nutritionist a necessary supply of vitamins for the malnourished population.

The driver took Victor straight to the American headquarters in the Kronprinzenallee in Dahlem. It was quite a long drive and gave him the time to go over his papers once again. Victor liked to be well prepared.

At the entrance gate to the Berlin Brigade he hopped off the French car, waved the driver good-bye and showed his badge to the guard. "General Harris is waiting for me."

He walked across the compound and then straight up the stairs to Harris' office. The secretary nodded and advised him, "Go right in. The general is waiting for you."

Victor nodded, opened the door and walked inside. He stood at attention near the doorway until Harris finished writing something. After saluting him, he walked forward, his hat beneath his arm.

"Sergeant Major Richards, thanks for coming over so quickly. Have a seat. Can I offer you a drink?"

"I'm fine, sir."

"Good." Harris cut right to the chase. "I'm flying to Wiesbaden this afternoon and want the most up-to-date information on the progress at Tegel."

"Sir, I'm happy to report that the imported machinery has worked wonders for productivity. We're about a week ahead of schedule and I'm confident we can keep to the inauguration date of December 1st."

Harris nodded. "I was counting on that, or I wouldn't have specifically asked for you to take over the project management. But I was hoping we could make a first landing on the new runway as early as late October."

"Sir?" Victor thought he'd misheard. Moving the finishing date forward by more than four weeks was impossible.

"I'm telling you this under the seal of secrecy. General Cannon has been appointed Commander-in-Chief of USAF Europe and will be leaving the United States by the end of October. He will want to visit Berlin and form his own opinion about Operation Vittles. It would be a nice touch to have him land at the new airport, don't you think so?"

Victor certainly thought so, but wasn't sure he could deliver on such a bold request. On the other hand, who was he to deny Harris and Cannon such an accomplishment? He took a deep breath and said, "Sir, I cannot guarantee that Tegel will be ready for regular operations by then, but the runway will be available to receive General Cannon's plane."

Harris smiled. "That's what I wanted to hear. You have not betrayed my faith in you." Then his expression hardened. "It doesn't look like the Russians are going to lift the blockade anytime soon. Diplomatic negotiations are stalled and Soviet fighters are buzzing our planes in the corridors. They're playing for time, hoping General Winter will defeat us the same way he defeated the Germans at the gates of Moscow in 1941. With winter coming, we not only have to fight against bad weather, but we'll need to fly in ten times more coal than during summer."

Victor had not considered this detail, but it made sense. In summer people didn't heat their houses and coal was only needed to cook or produce electricity.

Harris scrutinized him. "You work with many Germans in Tegel. How is the mood among them?"

"Sir, those I have talked to are grateful for what we do for them and are determined to hold out. They will not succumb to the communist propaganda and the lure of free bread." He thought of Bruni and her fervent disdain for the Russians. "In fact, I have it on good account that most West Berliners would rather starve than live inside the Russian bear's paw."

"That good account is a German *Fräulein*, I assume?"

"Yes." Victor felt his ears burning. He wasn't the only one with a German girlfriend, but he still felt guilty.

Harris leaned forward, resting his elbows on the desk. "There's nothing wrong with that. We abolished the non-fraternization policy long ago, but let me give you some advice from a man who's much older and more experienced than you. Most of the *Fräuleins* are only interested in their own benefit. Understandably, in the situation they are in. Dating an American has enough perks to make them put their moral standards aside. As long as you are aware this is a business relation and not true love, it can be beneficial for both sides. But if you expect her to love you, then you'll be most certainly disappointed. I've seen it happen more times than I care to count."

Victor didn't want to listen to this; it sounded too similar to what Bruni herself had told him. That she wasn't in this for love, but because they both profited from it. A beneficial exchange, she'd called it.

He hated to see it that way and hoped that with time she'd change her mind. But now Harris took the same line, shattering Victor's hopes for a common future with Bruni.

"Some of them are truly gorgeous and a nice pastime, but nothing more. Always keep this in mind."

"I will, sir." Logically, he knew he should heed Harris' advice. But his heart and his mind weren't anywhere close to being on the same page on this issue.

Dean continued, "Take my advice, son. Once you're back stateside, find yourself a nice American woman and settle down."

Victor pushed aside the advice and focused instead on the mention of his returning home. "Sir, may I ask when that might be?"

"Anxious to leave us, Sergeant Major?"

"Don't take this the wrong way, but in a word – yes."

"Well, as soon as Tegel is fully operational, I will personally sign your request for demobilization."

"I'm going to hold you to that promise." Victor's mind was already spinning with ideas as he contemplated finally shipping home. He wouldn't even complain if he'd have to board a plane to get there. He just wanted to go home. Maybe then he'd get Bruni out of his head – for good.

"One more thing," Harris said. "Can we go over the load-bearing capacity of the new runway again? Since both Tempelhof and Gatow are in increasingly bad shape, I'd like to shift the heavier planes to Tegel."

"Sure." Victor pulled several sheets of paper from his briefcase. He'd already calculated the materials needed and how much tonnage the runway could handle without being crushed. He had even foreseen the possibility of having bigger and heavier planes than currently existed. He wanted Tegel to be prepared for the next century.

When he left Harris' office, it was already late and he

sought out his quarters to take a shower and change into a fresh uniform. Then he decided to return to the French sector and visit Bruni at the cabaret. She might never love him, but with the prospect of leaving Germany by the end of this year, he'd comfort himself with happily sharing her bed every night until then.

28

BRUNI

Her heart jumped as she recognized Victor's familiar figure in the audience. She made eye contact with him and sang her next song exclusively for him.

During the break before her last performance, she casually passed by his table and told him to meet her later at the back entrance. Then she settled at a table with some British officers. It was important to be friendly with all of the patrons, while not favoring just one of them – at least not until she'd found herself a steady benefactor again. And even then, the men liked the illusion that Bruni loved all of them.

She swallowed a giggle. If only those fools knew that Brunhilde von Sinnen would never love anyone, because love made a woman weak and vulnerable. And Bruni was neither.

After the show Victor waited for her at the back door and greeted her with a passionate kiss on the mouth.

"Hello, gorgeous," he said when they had to come up for air, taking her arm.

"I had hoped to see you tonight," she answered with a voice full of promise. As much as she condemned the notion of true love and all that kitsch, she couldn't help but get wobbly knees in his presence, and against her better judgment was disappointed when he didn't show up two nights in a row.

Victor was fun to be with, with a great sense of humor, and he never missed an opportunity to compliment her beauty. Bruni knew she was vain, but it felt incredibly good when Victor told her she was the most beautiful woman on earth.

"How was your day?" she asked while he guided her to his car.

"Busy, but good. I met with General Harris – you must know how demanding he is."

Bruni gasped. Victor was working with Dean? Why hadn't she considered that possibility? And why did he assume she knew about Dean's imperious character?

A twinge of guilt washed over her, because she'd never told him that she and Dean had been a couple. But then she pushed the remorse away. It wasn't his business. She and Victor had a casual fling, nothing else. That certainly didn't give him rights to be privy to her past. She hadn't asked Victor about girls before her either, and since he was a soldier he must have had many. So why did she even feel this way?

To mask her turmoil she said in a matter-of-fact voice, "What did the Kommandant want from you?"

Victor chuckled. "Oh, nothing much, he just wants Tegel ready for the first plane to land by late October."

"That early? I thought the inauguration was planned for the first of December?"

Victor opened the passenger door and helped Bruni climb inside as gracefully as possible with her high heels and pencil skirt. He laughed, "Why don't you wear something more practical after work?"

Bruni glowered at him. "How would that look? I'm a goddess. Have you ever seen a goddess in dungarees and work boots?"

"In fact, I haven't, but I have seen her without clothes and she looks even better in the nude." Victor gave her a kiss and then walked around the car to hop in on the driver's side, while Bruni felt the heat searing through her body. She could barely wait to show him just how good this particular goddess looked when the two of them were lying on the bed, limbs entangled.

"Your place or mine?" Victor asked. It was a running joke between them, because there was no way he could bring her into the garrison.

"Mine." Bruni leaned back in the seat, letting the tension of the day fall off her shoulders. With Victor she always felt so good. Protected. Loved – no, scratch that, love didn't exist. Cherished.

"Sweetheart." His hand snaked on her thigh. "Would you mind accompanying me to Tempelhof airport? I need to pick up a box there. Or would you rather have me deliver you home first and come back later?"

She was tired and hungry, but she'd rather sit with him

in the car than be alone in her cold and dark place. "I don't mind."

"It won't take long." Victor was right. Fifteen minutes later he parked in front of Tempelhof airport. The airport was a restricted area, so he pecked her on the lips and said, "I'll be right back."

After several minutes waiting in the car, Bruni longed for a smoke, but as usual, didn't have a lighter with her. Reluctantly, she got out of the car and walked over to the sentry to ask him for a light, which he eagerly offered in exchange for one of her famous smiles.

She walked back to the car, watching the busy work on the airfield. Even now in the middle of the night, hundreds of people were milling about. The sky hung full of planes lined up like a string of pearls, their lights blinking and dancing, ready to land in ninety-second intervals, bringing essential goods to Berlin.

The loud droning of plane engines filled the air and Bruni watched in awe how another plane landed with spectacular precision, setting off a chain of events. Trucks were dispatched from the hangar and rushed toward the aircraft, dozens of men and women hopping out and unloading the entire cargo in a speed that reminded her of those Charlie Chaplin movies where they accelerated everything to double speed.

"Impressive, isn't it?" Victor had returned and put an arm around her shoulders.

"It is." She suddenly had tears in her eyes. A mere three years ago Victor's and her nations had been mortal enemies, and today the Americans and British were mounting the hugest airlift in the history of mankind, just to save people like herself from being crushed by the Soviet thugs. "You know, I never thought about it – for years we all lived in mortal fear whenever we heard the droning of a plane, but this has all changed in a few short months. Now, it's the best sound in the world and we get worried when the noise stops. It's almost like a lullaby, soothing and filled with so much hope. As long as the planes continue to land, we will persist."

In a sudden impulse, she slung her arms around him and pressed her cheek against Victor's chest. "Thank you so much for all of this."

He looked slightly confused and she explained, "At the cabaret the girls were worried about what will happen once winter comes. I mean we'll need coal for heating but with the airlift barely bringing in enough food, what happens when the coal supplies are used up? Will we all freeze to death?"

"That's why we're building Tegel. Once it's open we'll have almost double capacity, shifting the bigger planes to the new runway, which is the longest and sturdiest in all of Europe." He took her chin between his hands and added, "You have no reason to worry. General Harris said it himself, the Americans aren't going to let the Berliners starve at the hands of the Russians. And...I can't tell you what it is, but we have another ace up our sleeve, and that will make a tremendous difference once winter rolls in."

"I'm so glad you're here," she said and snuggled up against him, leaving it open whether she meant him or the Americans in general.

"You're not going to get rid of us anytime soon." He chuckled and pressed her tighter against him, and for once she was quite happy that he had no intention of ever leaving her side. "Let's go home."

Home? He considered her apartment home. A sudden fear grabbed Bruni's heart. Victor was such a nice guy, she didn't want to see him hurt when the inevitable day came and they had to end this casual fling, because she'd finally found herself a suitable man.

Captain Rublev came to her mind, and she all but broke into a giggle at the garbage he'd told her, which was repeated by the SED-owned newspaper *Neues Deutschland* day after day. The airlift was pure war-mongering on the part of the Western Allies and there was, in fact, no blockade. The Soviet Union provided for her people, the other Allies did not.

She could understand why a man like Rublev kept to the Soviet directives, but why had the SED sycophants sold their souls, country and compatriots to the Russians? What had they gotten in return? She couldn't fathom a bargain worth doing these soul-crushing things.

Bruni herself was an opportunist and had been the consort of a Russian captain. It had been a very beneficial relationship: she slept with him and he protected her from being raped. The perfect bargain in her eyes, but she'd never have agreed to selling out her own country, her friends, or her coworkers because of her relationship with him. She hadn't helped him spew lies and threats during the election campaign and she most certainly hadn't voted for the Russian-owned SED party.

No, she might be selfish, vain and always out for her own benefit, but she certainly wasn't a traitor.

"Hey, gorgeous, everything okay?" Victor's voice sounded worried.

"Yes. I'm just tired." She didn't want him to know how selfish a person she was, because Victor somehow hadn't been able to see her for what she really was and thought she was a wonderful, kind, and caring person. Let him believe in that illusion for a while longer.

"Do you want me to return to the garrison after dropping you off at your place?"

His face looked positively adorable when he was concerned about her, and a wave of warmth surged though her body. "No, I really want you to stay with me tonight."

"Then let's go. And then we can unpack this box."

"A gift, for me? What is it?"

"It's a surprise, therefore I can't tell you." His eyes twinkled with delight.

Bruni playfully punched his biceps. "Oh, you're so mean."

29

VLADI

General Sokolov's head looked like a tomato about to explode, not that tomatoes were something readily available in Berlin. At least the Western sector hadn't seen fresh produce since the traffic inspection roadblocks had started three months earlier.

"This isn't working the way you said it would," Sokolov yelled at the air forces commander, Colonel Ulyanin.

"We've been doing military exercises that include crossing the corridors, and we've even instructed our people to buzz their planes, but those stubborn capitalists simply won't give up. Not even the deadly accident last week, when one of our best fighters collided with one of their unannounced planes, caused them to reconsider their illegal activities over our territory."

Vladi wondered whether he had missed a new directive indicating the Western Allies had to announce planes using the corridor to the Soviet authorities, but in any case took note that going forward he'd have to mention that the

190

traffic in the corridors was illegal; maybe the corridors didn't even exist? He'd have to probe that issue later with Ulyanin, as he didn't want to enrage Sokolov with undue questions.

"Comrade Rublev, what intelligence have you got?" Sokolov shouted, his tomato-colored face transforming into a pained grimace.

He still called me Comrade, so I'm not yet on my way to Siberia. Vladi inhaled deeply, pondering whether to tell the general the good or the bad news first. If he started with the bad news, he risked being disposed of in a fit of rage, but on the other hand, if he could end his part on a good note, Sokolov might take mercy on him.

He opted for bending the truth. "Comrade General, we're making good progress."

"Your unit has been telling me this for weeks, so where are the facts?"

Probably the good news was needed more urgently at the moment. "The listening device opposite Gatow airport is fully functional and everything we're picking up is sent to Moscow immediately for decryption." Vladi didn't say that the British knew about the listening device and had taken extra measures to conceal important radio messages, while continuing to broadcast from tower to planes in clear text.

"And what information have we picked up?"

That was the problem. The experts in Moscow hadn't been able to break the encryption yet. "I'm awfully sorry, Comrade General, but I haven't been briefed on this top secret matter. I assume you'll be informed directly by Moscow."

Sokolov scowled. He wasn't stupid and probably saw

through Vladi's attempt to shift the blame to someone else, but he couldn't very well criticize anyone in Moscow for keeping information from a lowly captain.

Now Vladi needed all his instincts to frame the next, much worse, topic.

"Comrade General, apart from finally having a listening device to spy on the British, we have managed to plant several spies at the construction site in Tegel." Vladi meticulously avoided mentioning the word airport, as this would elicit another fit of rage. Ever since the Americans had started constructing the airport in the French sector, Sokolov's mood had deteriorated rapidly.

"Do you think I don't already know that?" Sokolov exploded and out of the corner of his eye, Vladi noticed how Colonel Ulyanin seemed to become one with the wall.

"Naturally, Comrade General, in your great wisdom you know all of this already, but," now it would be even harder to give him the bad news, "our spies have told us the Americans have been flying in heavy machinery like cranes and excavators and—"

"That's impossible!" Spittle flew from Sokolov's mouth.

Vladi intently stared at the toes of his shoes while answering, "I'm afraid they thought of a way to dismantle the equipment, fly it to Berlin and reassemble it here again."

"Those capitalists be damned! Why can't they return to where they came from and leave us in peace?"

Neither Vladi nor Ulyanin dared to give an answer to this obviously rhetorical question. But Vladi still needed to present the worst news of all. "Comrade General, our spies have mentioned the possibility that the construction might be finalized in less than six weeks."

He had not expected the violence of Sokolov's outburst. After cursing at them for a total of ten minutes and slamming his fists onto the oak desk with such force that his secretary peeked in looking like a frightened mouse, and then yelling for his anti-ulcer medicine, Sokolov finally glared at Vladi, making him feel as if the oxygen were being squeezed from his lungs.

"And this...just in time for winter. Do you know what this means?"

"Yes, Comrade General."

"It means they will increase their capacity by at least thirty percent, which more than makes up for the loss of the tonnage of the Sunderland seaplanes that cannot land on frozen water."

"Yes, Comrade General," Vladi whispered, fearing that Sokolov would strangle him with his bare hands.

"It means these beasts will have the capacity to fly in coal. And that means Berliners won't freeze, and that in turn means they won't flock to our administration offices where they can register their ration cards to get our coal and our food. And that means..." Sokolov stared silently at Vladi for a long time. "...if General Winter isn't on our side with plenty of fog and ice, then this blockade is doomed and we might as well stop bothering."

Vladi gulped. It was the first time Sokolov had used the word *blockade*. According to official language, blockade meant that an area was hermetically cordoned off, which was not the case for Berlin, because traffic from Berlin, both East and West, to the surrounding Soviet-occupied zone was still possible.

"And if this action doesn't bring the desired results, then

someone has to pay for it." Now Sokolov had an outright mean expression in his eyes. "And it won't be me."

Vladi believed he heard a gulp from Colonel Ulyanin, who'd been pressed against the wall, motionless, apparently hoping Sokolov would forget he was present.

Ulyanin snapped to attention. "Comrade General, we will double our efforts to intercept American and British air traffic and," he gave a pleading glance to Vladi, "we request the help of Red Army Intelligence to increase the pressure on the ground."

Sure, now the rat Ulyanin tried to pass the responsibility for this fiasco to Intelligence.

"Arrange some riots, or better yet, distract the Western Allies," Sokolov said. "Why don't you keep them occupied with some real problems so they won't have time for their air charade?"

Vladi's mind was running a mile a minute trying to come up with something. He slowly said, "Comrade General, if you allow, we could start a few diversions in the underground stations in the Western sectors." The entire S-Bahn system was guarded by East Berlin police. It would be one of his easiest tasks to have them wreak havoc. "I'm thinking of seizing all Western publications to start."

That would cause a veritable outcry among the Berliners and would keep the military police of all sectors busy – too busy to deal with attacks that might happen simultaneously at the Tegel site.

"Do whatever you want, but do it fast and get me results," Sokolov said in a slightly mollified tone.

"Thank you, Comrade General; if you'll allow, I'll get to it right away."

Sokolov merely waved a hand and Vladi felt as if someone had lifted a heavy burden from his shoulders. He saluted and fled Sokolov's office in a hurry. He was still alive and well – for now. But his next moves had better produced the desired results, if he didn't want to be the one to pay for the failed Operation "Traffic Inspections."

30

BRUNI

October had arrived, with colorful leaves falling from
the few trees that had survived the war. The beautiful yellow, orange and red hues were a welcome embell-
ishment of the otherwise gray and drab city.

But autumn had brought other, less welcome guests: low
temperatures, harsh Easterly gusts, long hours of darkness,
and fog. Frost covered the weeds and grass growing atop
the rubble heaps, and would only melt away around noon.

Low visibility was the worst enemy of the pilots.
Everyone in Berlin, Bruni included, became tense and bad-
tempered when the constant engine droning stopped. And
these days it stopped often, sometimes for twenty-four
hours on end.

Victor had explained to her how ground controlled
approach with radar talked the pilots down even during bad
weather periods, but when the fog became too thick, there
was nothing either the air traffic controller or the pilot
could do to ensure a safe landing.

Unfortunately, October had decided to bring lots and lots of the despised fog, interrupting the flights. As she walked to queue up for rations, Bruni rubbed her hands against the cold, imagining how the awful General Sokolov gleefully did the same, basking in this unexpected help.

Soon, winter would bear down on the city with snow and temperatures below freezing point, day and night. She remembered all too well the winter two years prior when nearly two thousand people in Berlin alone had frozen to death.

This year, each Berliner had been given a ration of one sack of coal for the entire winter. Bruni snorted. That would last three weeks at most. Thankfully she still owned the ostentatious fur coat Feodor had given her and the plush eiderdown, courtesy of Dean Harris.

What she was more worried about was food. The dehydrated vegetables being flown in tasted like barbed wire and nothing else was much better, not even the American army rations Victor provided. The only way to obtain fresh and tasty groceries was on the black market.

But since the Soviets had started an all-out war against black-marketeering and cracked down on trade between their zone and West Berlin, this had become increasingly dangerous. Even crossing into the Eastern part of Berlin, to buy goods on the open market there, was becoming difficult. West Berliners were habitually searched on their way home by Soviet soldiers, and if caught, the confiscation of all goods was the least of punishments.

Even Heinz had been arrested once, despite his good contacts among the Russian officials, and only a considerable bribe had bought him his freedom three days later. He'd left the prison with a limp and two missing teeth.

No, Bruni wasn't brave enough to go stockpiling in the Soviet zone. She rather made do with barbed-wire-tasting dried vegetables and the slightly less disgusting Army rations. At least the Café de Paris baked their own bread, and as an employee she received each evening a bowl of potato soup with two thick slices of heavenly smelling fresh bread.

Still, Bruni was concerned. Her dresses hung loosely around her hips and bosom and she worried that her female curves were beginning to succumb to the deficient diet. Her looks were her most precious capital, and without her ability to enchant her male audience she was as good as dead.

She gave a deep sigh and opened the back door to the cabaret. The kitchen was the only heated room, so the girls always came here first to warm up, catch up on gossip and hope for some leftovers from cooking.

"Hello, everyone," Bruni greeted the other employees.

"Have you read the news?"

Bruni shook her head. There was always some breaking news, but right now she was more interested in wrapping her hands around a mug of hot tea.

"The Magistrat has passed a resolution, against the vote of the SED, to allow cutting down the Grunewald," Gabi said.

Bruni shrugged. As far as she was concerned, they could chop up every damn tree if it would keep her warm. "Probably a wise thing to do, since there's not enough coal for heating."

"How can you say that?" Sally's eyes were glaring daggers. "The Grunewald is a beloved recreational area, one of the few pearls of beauty to survive the vicious Allied bombing. It's so sad."

Bruni's left eyebrow shot up. She'd never pegged Sally for a communist, and until today the woman had never once voiced her love for trees. "This really isn't the time to be nostalgic."

"You're a cold-hearted woman," Gabi said.

"Look, my heart might be cold, but my body needs heat. I'll miss the trees just like everyone else. But let's not forget why the Magistrat is doing this. It's because the Soviet assholes are blockading us and there's not enough coal to heat our homes in winter. I for my part don't want to turn into a block of ice."

Sally was spitting mad now. "The Soviets aren't assholes, in fact they are the only ones actually caring for our well-being. The *Neues Deutschland* newspaper said the Grunewald demolition is completely unnecessary, because the Soviets have generously offered to provide the Western sectors with enough coal, just like they've been doing with their sectors for years."

"Ah, and at what cost? What's our chip in the bargain?"

"Nothing. It's all between the four occupying powers."

The cook, a former Wehrmacht soldier with only one leg, raised his voice. "You're naïve, Sally. The price for the Soviet coal is to put the Ruhr area and its coal production under international government, enabling the Russians to steal as much of the production as they wish. Don't you ever read any newspaper besides *Neues Deutschland?*"

"It's not like that." Sally pursed her lips. "And...the poor lumberjacks don't even get proper tools. The puny axes and saws they're given aren't strong enough for the hardwood trees we have here."

Bruni wanted to laugh out loud, if it weren't so sad. Where did Sally get all this garbage news from? "That actually proves a point, right? If the Soviets didn't blockade Berlin, we could simply import the needed tools instead of having to make do with what we have." She gave her empty cup to the cook and turned around to change for her first performance, but Sally called after her. "There actually is no blockade, because that means an area is hermetically—"

Bruni couldn't listen to this nonsense a single second longer and began trilling the lyrics to one of her songs, effectively blocking out Sally's voice.

VICTOR

November 5, 1948

The big day had arrived and despite the fact that, apart from the runway, nothing else was fully functional at the new Tegel airport, the first aircraft was scheduled to land at exactly noon.

Victor, Pierre, James and the entire crew of French and American soldiers involved in the construction work lined the runway on the side next to the unfinished airport building and the control tower. On the other side of the runway stood thousands of curious German workers who didn't want to miss this significant moment in history. Everyone's faces gleamed with hopeful anxiety.

In the distance the sky was filled with approaching planes of all shapes and nationalities. Victor even spotted one with the Australian kangaroo emblem through his binoculars. Several minutes before noon, one plane broke out of the formation and took course toward them.

"That's them!" Victor was nervous. He, Pierre and James had tested everything a million times, but now it was for real. The aircraft chosen to make the first touchdown at Tegel was a Douglas C-54 Skymaster flown by Captain Glenn Davidson, carrying important passengers: United States Air Force Europe commander-in-chief General Cannon and the chief-of-staff of the American-British airlift, General Tunner.

Everything had to be perfect.

They couldn't have chosen a better day, because the sun was shining and not a single cloud darkened the clear blue sky. Exactly at noon, the big bird landed elegantly on the new tarmac and came to a complete stop about a hundred yards before the end of the runway.

The two generals stepped out and Victor hurried to salute them and give them a tour through the new buildings, before a driver took them to the American headquarters to confer with Generals Clay and Harris.

Meanwhile the cargo team jumped into their trucks and unloaded the huge bird in exactly twelve minutes, while the crew sauntered over to the mobile canteen and flirted with the *Fräuleins* handing out hot beverages and sandwiches.

Twenty minutes later, the Skymaster was back in the air, headed for Wiesbaden. Victor and Pierre retreated into their trailer, debriefing the team of air controllers and ground crew.

Sovereignty for Tegel airport would lie with the French army, who also coordinated the German workers and the dispatch of goods, while the Americans would oversee the flight operations, including air traffic control. They were confident of being able to start regular operations within two days.

But it never came to that.

The next day, Victor drove to Tempelhof airport to pick up radio equipment. He looked up when one of the pilots came walking toward the hangar.

They weren't supposed to do that, because for efficiency reasons they had to stay next to their planes. Victor groaned when he recognized the young man sauntering across the tarmac. Naturally, it had to be Glenn.

"Hey, man, how's life in Berlin?"

"Bed of roses, that is if you like the sound of the Soviet military doing exercises lulling you to sleep." The Germans weren't the only ones frightened by the Soviet military presence encircling Berlin. The hidden threat was grating on everyone's nerves and even General Harris had become skittish at the sound of exploding artillery shells next to the American garrison.

"Come on, can't be that bad. I hear there are a lot of pretty *Fräuleins* desperate to please an American soldier." Glenn chuckled. "Shame they won't let us into the city."

"I'm sure there are plenty of *Fräuleins* to bed in Wiesbaden, too." Victor turned around to inspect the contents of another wooden box cleverly labeled *Tegel*. "I have no idea which kind of genius over there does the labeling of the boxes," he murmured, already having forgotten about Glenn.

"Sorry, man, I'm actually here to deliver a letter. It's for a girl working at the Café de Paris. Do you know where that is?"

Victor's ears perked up. "Everyone does. Who's it for?"

"Some singer called Brunhilde von Sinnen."

"You know her?" Jealousy attacked Victor with unprecedented force and he hoped Glenn wouldn't divulge any intimate details of a past relationship with Bruni, or he'd have to beat the living daylights out of him.

"Not me. But one of the girls I'm trying to bed is a friend of hers."

The tension left Victor's body and he sagged with relief. "I can see that she gets the letter; the Café de Paris is not far from Tegel."

A loud whistle sounded and Glenn shrugged. "I have to get back, those bastards unload the cargo so fast, we don't even have the time for a piss." Then he produced an envelope from his pocket and handed it to Victor. "Promise you'll get it to Zara's friend? Or I'll never get a chance to bang her."

"No worries, I'll do it personally tonight. Wouldn't want to risk ruining your sex life."

Glenn slapped him on the back. "Thanks, man."

Victor was on the drive back to Tegel when the deluge of rain started. He dashed through the forming puddles, hoping to arrive in time before the ground in front of the construction trailer had turned into a mud-filled mess. He parked the car in front of the tower and rushed inside.

"Hey, Bob and Steve, I got the box with the radio equipment. Lend me a hand, will you?"

The two mechanics had been waiting for him and together they heaved the heavy box up the stairs, where the air controllers had their working space.

"I'll see you guys tomorrow, when we start regular operations," he said and then left the building again. Fortunately the rain had eased up. After returning the jeep to the construction trailer and telling Pierre that he was gone for the day, he walked the fifteen minutes from Tegel to Bruni's apartment, the letter from Zara tucked in his breast pocket. He distantly remembered a black-haired beauty looking much like Snow White for whom Bruni had given a farewell party on his first day in Berlin. Shamefully, he had to admit that he'd been too smitten with Bruni to pay much attention to her friend, but it was probably a fair guess that this was the same person.

On his way the rain stopped completely, but now the clouds descended, shrouding the Berlin sky in a thick fog. He looked up, missing the constant noise of the engines, and shook his head. Hopefully by tomorrow the visibility would be sufficient to fly again.

He knocked on the door and Bruni opened it with a huge smile, in a very figure-hugging dress. His mouth went dry and he felt his groin tighten. He certainly could never get enough of this woman. But before he swept her up in his arms and devoured her, he remembered his mission.

"I have a letter for you." He held her at arm's length and retrieved the envelope. "A pilot from Wiesbaden gave it to me."

Bruni frowned as she took the letter, but then she opened it and squealed in delight. "It's from Zara!"

"I take it Zara is a friend?" he said with a smile as she carefully opened the envelope.

Bruni nodded. "The best friend. She's a wonderful person and Marlene and I were so worried about her, because we haven't had word from her since she left Berlin. With the blockade and everything…I hope she's well."

The apartment was dark, save for the light of two candles, and Victor settled on the couch, giving Bruni the time to read the letter on her own. He loved watching her all the time, but when she wasn't aware of being watched, her entire body softened and her face lost the guarded expression.

Right now, her cheeks glowed in the dim candlelight. As she read, her expressive face turned worried, aghast, sad and finally relieved. He wondered what news the letter held to evoke such a reaction from her.

She dropped the letter into her lap and turned her head to look at him. "Thank goodness, Zara is fine." Tears welled up in her eyes. "You won't believe the horrific experience she had with the Russians, I can't imagine how she's still alive and kicking."

Victor scooted over and wrapped his arm around her shoulders. It was the first time he'd seen her cry, since Bruni normally was as emotional as a block of ice. It scared the living daylights out of him, but also endeared her more to him. Despite pretending not to be able to love, she must dearly love her friend Zara if she broke out in tears about a past ordeal, one that her friend had safely weathered.

Bruni's shoulders quivered as she continued to sob uncontrollably in Victor's arms, until she suddenly pushed him away and glowered at him with the hate of the entire world in her eyes. "I hate the Soviets for what they've done to her. Believe me, one day they will pay for this!"

"Sweetheart, please, calm down."

Bruni shook her head and said, "How can I calm down? Here, read for yourself."

Victor took the letter, feeling slightly uncomfortable for intruding on Zara's privacy, but the discomfort quickly turned into the urgent need to vomit and then to full-blown rage. It there had been a Russian nearby, he might have punched him to death.

Zara's letter was deliberately vague without giving sordid details, but he'd seen enough awful things during the war to fill in the blanks.

"She's safe now in Wiesbaden and that's all that counts." Victor kept stroking Bruni's back, trying to sooth her pain.

"It's all my fault!" Bruni said with a defeated voice.

"How can it be your fault?"

"Because I encouraged her to travel to Wiesbaden. If she hadn't been on that train…" Bruni flopped back on the couch, covering her face with her hands.

"She's probably been targeted, and they would have arrested her in Berlin, too."

"Not if she had stayed in the American sector."

"Despite the best efforts of our military police, the Soviets still sneak their cronies inside and abduct German citizens in cloak-and-dagger operations." Victor saw that his words weren't having any effect and felt completely helpless. Therefore he did the only thing that occurred to him and kissed Bruni on the mouth.

She desperately clung to him, returning his kiss until they were both breathless.

"Take me to the bed," she asked and he gladly obeyed, swooping her up in his arms and carrying her into the bedroom. Their love-making was even more passionate than usual, and for the first time he sensed that he'd gotten a glimpse at the raw, unadulterated, unrestrained version of Bruni, the one she so carefully kept hidden from anyone except her best friends.

Much later Bruni snuggled up against him, dragging the plush eiderdown over their bodies. "Thank you. I really needed this."

"It was my pleasure." Victor smiled. She might not have realized that tonight she had revealed her true self to him. It made him incredibly happy. Much more than it should.

"Zara has offered a place to stay for Marlene and me should we ever need to leave Berlin." She turned in his arms and her wonderful bright blue eyes filled with nostalgia. But her next question hit him unprepared: "Is that even possible?"

"What?" Victor wasn't completely sure what she expected from him.

"Getting out. Of Berlin. Is that even a possibility?"

"Not really. You'd need a special pass to travel on one of the departing planes and they are very few and terribly hard to come by." What he didn't add was that General Harris had full control of such passes and he'd never given one to a normal German citizen before. He'd even forbidden the wives and children of American soldiers to be flown out, because the Soviets would consider this a weakness and exploit it in their propaganda.

The only persons leaving Berlin, except for the important visitors and journalists coming to see the situation in Berlin with their own eyes, were high-ranking military like Harris himself or Berlin politicians on duty travel.

The British, though, had started to fly out hundreds of

the most undernourished children to be taken care of by their relatives in the Western zones for as long as the blockade lasted. But Bruni wasn't a child and despite having lost several pounds, certainly not undernourished.

She sighed. "I'm not talking about right now, but what if the Americans leave Berlin, could you get me out?"

He was moved by her request, although it was quite selfish of her. "Sweetheart, both General Harris and General Clay have promised not to throw the Berliners to the wolves. Even President Truman has said 'We are in Berlin and we will stay. Full stop.' You have no reason to be worried."

Bruni bit her lower lip. "But what if the Soviets start shooting down your planes?"

"They won't, because that means war. And they want a new war even less than we do."

"I'm not so sure about that."

"Sweetheart, there's no reason to worry. Really." He looked into her eyes, which were so full of anguish that he couldn't resist adding, "In the highly unlikely case that we're leaving Berlin, I'll find a way to get you out."

"Promise?" Bruni's eyes lit up with newfound hope.

"Promise." He had no idea how he'd pull that off, but he relied on the fact that it would never come to that.

BRUNI

The fog persisted.

Bruni was grateful for her fur coat as she braved the horrendous weather with heavy fog, ice, and sleet. Due to the bad conditions, public transportation had completely ceased to exist, but what was worse, so had air traffic.

For ten days in a row no planes had been able to land. The tension in the city was palpable, and even ever-optimistic Victor wore a sour face. She knew he was in a hurry to start operations at his airport, but so was everyone else.

"Hey, Bruni, you look awful. Here, take that." The cook handed her a bowl of hot soup as she arrived at the Café de Paris with her hair in a complete mess.

"Thank you. I wish winter was over already."

He laughed. "It's not even started yet. But have you heard? Sokolov is going to address the population on radio."

"What lies does he want to tell us this time?" Bruni shrugged. It was wasted time to hope for a modicum of human decency from the Soviets.

Elections for the city government were coming up fast and increased the existing tensions between East and West further. General Sokolov had graciously agreed to allow elections in all of Berlin, but under the condition that anti-democratic organizations like the trade union confederation and the cultural organization, both located in Eastern Germany and forbidden in the Western part, would be certified for the city elections.

Bruni had an inkling that this was another of Sokolov's fake concessions, because he knew very well that the Western Allies would never agree. When the Lord Mayor announced that those conditions were nothing but chicanery, the Soviets promptly replied by dragging him and several other high-ranking German politicians in front of a Soviet military tribunal and accusing them of warmongering.

She almost spilled her coffee when she'd heard it on the radio. The very people who held relentless and unnecessary field maneuvers next to the borders of the Western sectors in Berlin and constantly buzzed American and British planes in the corridors – they accused people who called them out on wanting to undermine free elections of warmongering?

"Shush," one of the waitresses said and turned the radio louder.

General Sokolov said a few words of greeting in German, and then handed it over to the radio announcer to read the prepared speech.

"To all men, women and children living in Berlin, especially in the American, British and French sectors. Moscow has not forgotten about you. We have seen your suffering."

"A suffering you caused," someone mumbled.

"We are extending a hand of friendship to you. We know the Western Allies cannot feed you. Their supply planes have stopped coming and soon, their troops will be pulling out. Inventory of coal has already run out and so has milk to give to your babies. But you need not despair, and your children don't have to starve, because the Soviet people are offering you, our brothers and sisters, the food your oppressors deprive you of."

"Oh my god, this is truly stage-worthy!" Bruni exclaimed, only to be shushed. Everyone in the room was riveted to the radio, listening to what the Soviet Kommandant had to say.

"We're calling to all good mothers who don't want their children to die, we're calling to the honest workers who want to provide for their families, and we're calling to every Berliner who stands on the side of peace, all of you are invited to register with the authorities in the Eastern sector. You will receive a loaf of bread and ration cards that allow you to buy produce in any of our plentifully stocked shops."

"But where's the catch?" Gabi asked.

"The catch is that once you're registered in the East you cannot vote anymore, because only the Western sectors have allowed free elections," Cook said.

"Pah. Who cares about elections when you're dead? I for my part already registered with the Soviets. Best decision I ever made," Sally said.

"How could you?" Bruni stared at her in disbelief, but Sally simply shrugged.

"I have a toddler to feed. You heard the Kommandant,

the Americans have no milk for our babies. Do you really want me to see my darling die over stupid politics?"

"Sokolov was lying," the cook said. "The Café can't buy milk, because the Americans give it only to families with children under three years of age. My nephew works in the warehouse at Gatow. There are enough supplies to feed all of us for at least twenty days."

"And then? What happens after the twenty days?" a young blonde girl, called Clara, asked.

"Then we start to worry." Cook was his usual phlegmatic self. Bruni guessed he'd seen worse during his days in the Wehrmacht.

"By then it will be too late to do anything!" Clara cried, big tears running down her face. "I have a baby to feed!"

"Clara, you need to calm down..."

The young woman was hysterical by this point and scrubbed her face before shaking her head. "I have to do this. This is my only chance. You don't expect me to kill my own child, now do you?"

Bruni thought the girl was being overly dramatic. Cook was probably right. And if push came to shove, Clara could still come groveling to the Soviets. They all still had this last option.

After Clara had gone, a silence fell over the small group, until someone murmured, "Poor mite."

33

VICTOR

Victor wasn't the only one completely stressed out. Even the otherwise completely laid-back Pierre exploded at every little issue and shouted at the French soldiers and German workers alike.

Victor looked at the calendar in the construction trailer and marked another day off. "Goddammit! Fifteen fucking days since the last plane landed!"

"I need that new welding device." James lit a fresh cigarette with the old one and blew smoke into the air. In the last days his chain-smoking had taken on superhuman dimensions, and Victor half expected him to start putting one cigarette in each corner of his mouth.

"And I need steel for the tower and ..." Victor ran a hand through his hair. Still, if the weather didn't get any better real soon, they would have worse problems than not finishing the airport buildings. Two million starved or frozen people, for example.

Exasperated, he left his desk and stepped out into the

cold, thick and impenetrable fog, barely able to see his own hand in front of his eyes. He knew the crew was testing the runway lamps at this very moment, but not a sliver of light penetrated through the thick mist.

Walking to the almost finished tower more by memory than by sight, he wished for the crisp and clear Eastern winds to sweep away the awful fog. Their absence was both a boon and bane for Berlin: on one hand the winds would bring clear sight, but on the other hand they would also bring snow and ice. It was only thanks to the mild temperatures that people hadn't frozen to death.

Yet, he still hoped for the weather to clear, because then the planes could bring in the much needed food and coal. It really was a lose-lose situation and everything was the Soviets' fault. He balled his fists, raising them up to his face as if fighting against an invisible Russian.

Even though the American garrison didn't suffer from the same shortages as the German civilians, the continual dreary darkness that the Berliners called "November" was depressing every last person.

Coming himself from rural Montana he was used to harsh winters with plenty of snow, but the impenetrable fog and the lack of artificial lights, due to power shortages, grated on his nerves.

Winter in Berlin was bitter. If Bruni was to be believed, and she rarely exaggerated, last season had been exceptionally cruel and thousands of Berliners had frozen to death. So maybe, the fog was preferable.

Once or twice a day an especially reckless pilot braved the elements and made it through the gray soup to land safely. Approaches to Gatow had a slightly higher chance of success, because landing out there was so much easier than at Tempelhof, which lay smack dab in the middle of Berlin.

In all this muddled mess, General Harris had taken a momentous decision and ordered coal to be exclusively flown in at the expense of food, because people could go a few days without food, but would freeze within hours without coal.

Not everyone agreed with his decision, of course, but Victor did. He still briefed General Harris twice a week about the non-progress at Tegel, and every time he entered Harris' office, he found the general bent across maps, charts and calculations, tweaking and tinkering with the needs of a starving population.

Harris' team had calculated the needed calories for subsistence down to the last digit, and they regularly thought up clever ways to save cargo space and weight in order to fly in more nutritional value with the same number of planes.

Four thousand tons a day were the absolute minimum needed to keep two million people alive – just barely. But a severe winter would inevitably cause calamities.

Victor saw the fear of a prolonged spell of bad flying weather etched into the general's face and with every day that passed, the threat of having to cut rations became more prominent.

It would be disastrous.

But Harris never gave up hope, and Victor didn't either. According to the German workers at Tegel, there'd never in history been a year when the November fog didn't dissolve as December approached. He prayed they were right.

On the other hand engineers in Wiesbaden and back in

the States were frantically working at a better and more powerful radar system that would finally enable aircraft to touch down in virtually any weather. Then they'd thumb their noses at the Soviets and their criminal, inhuman blockade.

Two days later, the mist lifted and the planes were finally coming in again. As the first cluster touched down at all three airports, Victor could hear the sigh of relief going through the city.

Operations at Tegel proceeded at full capacity with only minor glitches and Victor's work in Berlin was all but done. It was a wonderful elated feeling, but at the same time, nostalgia crept into his bones. Leaving Berlin would also mean leaving Bruni and despite his best intentions, he'd fallen hard and fast for her.

During one of his phone briefings he asked General Tunner about the next steps.

"Richards, you've done a great job with Tegel and I haven't forgotten about your request to return stateside, but I'd like you to stay on until the end of the year to make sure operations continue without a glitch."

"Yes, sir." Victor was disappointed and happy at the same time.

"General Harris has proposed giving you another promotion for Tegel's official inauguration, so you can return home a second lieutenant."

"Thank you, sir." Victor felt pride over his achievement, and the unexpected second promotion in such a short time. But he wasn't entirely happy.

He should be. Bruni had made it very clear that she was after an officer, not an enlisted man, and now he'd be an officer. In an attack of stubbornness, he decided not to tell her. If she didn't love him for what he was, she didn't deserve to know about his imminent promotion.

"Is that possible?" Tunner's voice brought him back to the present.

"I'm very sorry, sir, but the line was dead for about ten seconds. Would you be so kind as to repeat what you said?"

Tunner informed him about the plans for the upcoming official inauguration of Tegel airport and gave him instructions on what kind of event he expected for the invited guests.

"Yes, sir, that will be no problem at all. Now that construction is done, we can use the resources to prepare for inauguration, while still keeping operations at maximum capacity."

"Well. I'll see you there in a week." Tunner disconnected the line, leaving Victor in a peculiar state of anxiety.

In a week from now his baby would officially be presented to the world, and he'd receive a promotion. And four weeks after that, he'd be on his way back to the States.

It was a dream come true, except for one tiny thing...

BRUNI

Bruni was both excited and nervous. Today was the inauguration day for the Tegel airport and Victor had arranged for her and Marlene to receive a special invitation. The acting Lord Mayor Louise Schröder would be giving a speech, along with the three Kommandanten Generals Harris, Ganeval and Herbert.

The chief-of-staff of the Anglo-American airlift, General Tunner, would also attend the event. In a drab and subdued city, it was a welcome opportunity to celebrate.

She pondered for a while on which dress to wear and then opted for a simple, figure-hugging dark green ensemble, with a fitted jacked and a slim skirt ending an inch beneath her knee. She could have chosen something flashier, but thought it appropriate to show austerity in a city stricken with shortages of everything.

To make up for the simple dress she styled her platinum curls around her face and used every trick in the book to make her eyelashes appear longer and thicker, while carefully avoiding the theatrical look she used on stage.

This was her opportunity to introduce herself as a respectable woman, a beloved entertainer in the likes of her idol Marlene Dietrich. A woman even the highest brass wanted to be acquainted with publicly.

It was something that had rankled her for quite a while. All the officers she knew, except for Feodor, had dated her more or less in secret, never acknowledging her publicly. Even Victor, who'd fallen in love with her like a puppy, had not come out and presented her as his official girlfriend.

That's the way you wanted it, no strings attached, remember? her inner voice said.

Yes, that had been her way of life for so many years, but during the past months Victor had chipped away the ice around her heart piece by piece, slowly melting her determination to see him as purely a *business arrangement*.

She sighed and applied soft pink lipstick to her lips. It was nice to dream of true love, but it would only get her hurt in real life. The moment you believed in a man, he exploited and used you. No, she had no intention of gluing herself together after another shattered heart.

With that thought in mind, she put on a matching hat, grabbed gloves, coat and handbag, and was giving herself a last once-over in front of the mirror when someone knocked on the door.

"Hello, Marlene." Bruni air-kissed her on both cheeks. Marlene wore her best dress, a hand-me-down from Bruni, and looked as excited as Bruni felt.

"You look absolutely stunning, so...statesmanlike. You could easily be our next Lord Mayor," Marlene greeted her.

"Goodness no! Listening to boring discussions all day long in the Magistrat is not my cup of tea."

Marlene laughed. "That's your idea of what a Lord Mayor does?" Then she looked around. "Isn't Victor coming?"

"No, he can't pick us up, because he's been busy overseeing last-minute preparations since early morning. We'll have to walk, it's only twenty minutes."

"I have no idea how you can walk such a distance in those," Marlene said with a pointed gaze from her sturdy shoes to Bruni's high heels.

"Practice. Now let's go."

On the way to the airport they caught up on gossip, wondering how Zara was faring in Wiesbaden and whether this pilot who'd given the letter to Victor was her boyfriend or not.

"No, that's so not like Zara," Marlene said. "You know how much she dislikes a uniform."

"She may dislike the uniform, but if the man inside is charming her pants off, why would she resist?"

"Come on, Bruni, not everyone is like you."

Bruni laughed. "I sure would hope they aren't. Because that would make a right mess of our world, wouldn't it?"

"Talking about men, what about you and Victor?" Marlene said it lightly, but Bruni sensed the deeper meaning behind her words.

"You know me. There's nothing serious between us. He's not really my type and like all the soldiers he probably has a wife back home."

Marlene stopped in her tracks and all but shouted, "You haven't asked him?"

Bruni had asked him, but she would not admit this. "Why should I? There's nothing emotional between us, this is purely a relationship of convenience."

"I don't believe you." Marlene shrugged and began walking again.

"Whatever makes you think I suddenly changed my ways and am eating my heart out for a man?"

"Because of the way your voice goes soft when you talk about him and how you look at him. You may fool yourself, but you can't fool me, Fräulein von Sinnen! You and I have been friends for much too long."

Bruni wasn't ready to even consider the option that Marlene might be on to something, so she quickly changed the topic. "With three airports within the city limits, do you think the Americans will be able to feed us throughout winter?"

Marlene shrugged as if to say that she wouldn't dig deeper if Bruni didn't want to talk about Victor and then said, "I sure hope so. And let's pray that General Winter has switched sides." There was a running joke in Berlin about the three undefeated generals: Polish General Mud, Russian General Winter, and American General Distance.

They arrived at the airport, presented their invitations, and were shown to the cordoned-off area for press and visitors. Bruni didn't care much about the speeches and all the praise for everyone involved and was quite happy when the official part ended and she spotted Victor approaching them.

He shook first Marlene's hand and then hers, giving her the devastating smile that always made her knees go weak, but he didn't kiss her. Bruni's heart tightened.

"How did you like the event?" he asked.

"It was wonderful and you can't imagine how grateful everyone in Berlin is for what the Americans are doing for us!" Marlene replied gracefully, but Bruni merely shot him an angry glance.

Victor bent forward and whispered in Bruni's ear, "I'm sorry, gorgeous, that I couldn't pick you up."

Did he actually think that was the reason she was angry with him? Maybe a bit, but it definitely wasn't the main reason.

"There's a small reception with food, and you're invited," Victor said to both of them.

Marlene grinned. "If there's food I'm game."

Bruni wanted to scowl but refusing an invitation for food would have been outright dumb, so she mustered a smile and followed him.

After about half an hour rubbing shoulders with all the important people in Berlin, Victor sidled up to her and whispered, "Let's get out of here."

She looked at him and the loving expression on his handsome face wiped her disappointment away. "You don't have to stick around?"

"No. I'd rather be with you."

Bruni's heart sped up and warmth surged through her veins. She said goodbye to Marlene and less than half an hour later, she and Victor burst into her small apartment, hungry for each other.

"Do you want something to drink?" she asked.

Victor shook his head and stalked her toward the bedroom door. "I think you know what I want."

Bruni loved the teasing light in his eyes; she waved him

forward with a come-hither motion. "I do indeed." She hummed a melody as she moved about the room, removing piece after piece of clothing, until she stood there in only her high heels, underwear, and stockings held up by garters and a garter belt.

"Gorgeous," Victor whispered against her skin as he pulled her into his arms. "I want to remove the rest."

Bruni nodded and wrapped her arms around his neck as he carried her over to the bed.

Much later, Bruni was lying in his arms, thinking that maybe she should reevaluate her no-emotional-attachment rule. She'd never been in love before, but what she felt for and with Victor had to be close. It was unlike anything she'd ever experienced before.

"You awake?" she asked into the darkness.

"Yes. I can't sleep."

Victor ran a hand down her back and then sighed, bringing Bruni's head up to look at him. "What's wrong?"

"The airport is finished."

"You did a great job," she beamed at him. "I was very proud of you today."

"Thanks. I had an agreement with General Tunner. He'll sign my demobilization paperwork as soon as my work here is finished." His voice sounded strained.

It took a moment for his words to sink in and when they did, Bruni felt as if her world was falling apart. "You're leaving?"

"By the end of the month. I'm being transferred back to the States."

Bruni scrambled away from him, grabbing the eiderdown and wrapping it tightly about herself. "I can't believe you're doing this to me!"

Victor sat up and shoved a hand through his hair. The moonlight was coming through the window, but other than that, all she could see of him was his silhouette. He slid from the bed and fumbled about until he found the matches and the candles.

"Bruni, I need you to listen to me. You knew this day would come."

Bruni had fled from the bed and was standing near the window, her shoulders shaking with fury. He took a step toward her, but she turned on him, fire coming from her eyes. "Just leave me alone."

"Why are you so upset? You don't care for me, not really. Remember?"

Bruni picked up a shoe lying on the floor and threw it at him. "Get your things and get out."

"You're asking me to leave in the middle of the night?"

"Yes. Now. I don't want you here, ever again." She knew she was being irrational, but after finally coming to grips with the fact that she was having true feelings for him, he abandoned her! She'd known it all along! All men were the same! Give them your heart and they trampled on it.

35

VICTOR

Victor was dumbstruck. Since it was she who'd always insisted theirs was merely a relationship of convenience and had nothing to do with true emotions, he wasn't prepared for such a violent reaction.

She'd known all along that he would leave Berlin after the airport was finished – to Wiesbaden or the States, what difference did it make? In a blockaded city any distance was insurmountable.

With a confused glance at the furious woman standing at the window and glaring daggers at him he quickly gathered up his clothing and left the bedroom, using the kitchen to get dressed again. She wasn't a good markswoman, but he wouldn't want to risk her throwing the second one of her shoes at him and by chance hitting him with that vicious heel.

He was angry, but more with himself than with her. He'd thought telling her about his leaving would be a relief. But she had acted like a jilted lover. His mind mused over the happenings and it wasn't until he was completely dressed and already had his hand on the doorknob, when the reason for her anger finally registered. *She's in love with me.*

The shock over this revelation punched him right in the gut and he sank onto the dilapidated chair, staring at the empty wall. *She's in love with me.* Those words rolled around in his head over and over again.

Despite her refusal to see the obvious, there was no denying it anymore. A lazy smile crept over his face until it spread from ear to ear. Bruni was completely different from what he'd imagined he wanted in a woman, but hell, did he love her!

He eyed the apartment door but leaving seemed like giving up. If there was one thing Victor never did, it was to give up without a good fight. Apparently it was time to fight for what he wanted. Bruni.

Without a proper plan for what to tell her, he got up and returned to the bedroom. He knocked on the door, but she didn't answer so he turned the knob and the scene in front of him broke his heart. That gorgeous woman lay across the bed, her face buried in a pillow, her hands fisted in the sheets, as she cried. Over him.

He walked over and put a hand on her back. "Sweetheart, please, stop crying and talk to me."

"Why are you still here?" she sniffed into the covers.

"Because I care and I didn't want to leave. Talk to me, please?"

"You said everything there was to say." She sat up, putting some distance between them.

"Not hardly." He reached for her and hauled her onto his

lap, ignoring her protests. "I didn't realize how much you cared for me."

"I don't."

"Yes, you do, or you wouldn't be so upset. I'll even go first if that will make it easier." Victor turned her head up to face him, used his thumbs to wipe her tears away and then kissed her softly. "I love you. I have for a while now, but I was afraid to tell you. Afraid that you would laugh at me, because you always said I was just another pleasant distraction and that your heart could never belong to a man."

Bruni looked at him and then blushed. "I said those words, because I've always thought that way. But then you came along…the whole thing frightened me. I'm not really good at emotions. I'm sorry."

"Don't be." Victor's heart was jubilant, but he needed to hear it from her. "Does that mean you feel something for me?"

She nodded and then cupped his cheek. "I think I love you. The thought of never seeing you again tore my heart apart. If that's love, then I love you." He dropped his head and kissed her with all of the passion in his soul.

"So, where do we go from here?" he asked once they had to come up for air.

"I don't know." Her eyes misted over with despair.

"Come with me!"

"How would that work? If you haven't noticed there's a blockade going on."

He couldn't help but chuckle. That was his girl; she never lost her dry humor.

"Well, yes, that's a small problem, but…" A thought

occurred to him. There was really just one way around this. But were they both ready for such a momentous decision?

He looked at her beautiful face, her shimmering blue eyes and suddenly remembered the story of an American soldier who'd married a German, taken her back to the States, just to find out that she had already a husband waiting there for her.

Following his gut, he said, "I can ask to stay in Berlin, but then I would forego the promised promotion I'd receive once I return to the States." It was a clever way to find out whether she would stick by his side while he was still rank and file.

"I can't possibly expect you to do this," she said, snuggling tighter against him. "You've been waiting for this promotion so long, and you deserve it so much. Without you, Tegel would still be a dream!"

"You are my dream come true." He kissed her again.

She squinted her eyes at him. "Are you saying this simply to make yourself feel less guilty for leaving me in this cursed city?"

That accusation came as a surprise. "Me? No. I really want to be with you. I love you."

Bruni seemed unconvinced, which was mystifying – to him, at least. After pretending not to care for him all this time, now she believed he was toying with her? What kind of warped mindset was this?

"Sweetheart. That's not at all the case, believe me."

She pushed away from him. "Whenever a man says 'believe me' he's lying."

Victor wanted to howl with desperation. "What can I do to show you that I'm serious and mean what I say?"

"Do something outrageous for me."

"Like what?"

"I don't know." Bruni shrugged her shoulders. "Something that is hard, but not impossible."

Victor thought for a moment and then he grinned. "I might have an idea…since you're always complaining about the Russian propaganda, what if I silenced their radio station – just for you."

Her eyes became wide as saucers. "That's impossible." Then she cocked her head and scrutinized him. "You're serious, aren't you?"

"Very."

"Well. If you manage to silence the Soviet radio, even for just one day…" She traced her tongue enticingly across her lips and Victor would have liked to take her right there and then again. "…then I'll believe that you truly love me and I'll do whatever it takes to be with you. Even if that means living on a farm in rural Montana for the rest of my life." She scrunched up her nose in disgust and he couldn't help himself, but pushed her on her back and placed kisses all over her skin.

"It's a deal," he said before making love to her one more time.

VLADI

Vladi smacked his forehead on the bar top in one of the shadier places in Berlin, where he'd been drinking all day.

"Bloody son of a bitch! He did it!" he cursed, wondering whether this day could become any shittier. The Westerners had their third airport fully functional, sunshine and winds had lifted the impenetrable fog, and to top it all off, the Americans had just announced a new record tonnage being flown in.

Wallowing in self-pity he wanted to order another vodka, when two of his comrades from Red Army Intelligence burst through the door and came straight up to him.

"Hey, Vladi, you're needed in Karlshorst," his old pal Grigori said and motioned for the other man, Alexej, to grab him by the arm. Together they dragged him out of the bar and to the waiting car.

"Hell, man, it's not even dinnertime yet and you're a

drunken wreck. What's wrong with you?" Grigori scolded him, while Alexej smirked.

"My life's over. Bloody American finished his airport. Weather is on their side too, and now they're licking the blocka— traffic controls." He really should keep his mouth shut.

"Get your shit together, or you won't see the end of this day." Grigori held Vladi's chin up with one hand and at his nod, Alexej dumped a bucket of ice-cold water over his face.

"Goddamn bastards. Are you trying to drown me?" Vladi swallowed and spluttered.

"On the contrary, trying to save your sorry ass. General Sokolov wants to talk to you."

Well, wasn't that just swell? He could barely keep his thoughts coherent and was summoned before the general. This was his unique chance to speed up his banishment to Siberia. At least he'd meet quite a few former colleagues in the gulags there. Vladi gave a coughing laugh. "What's he want?"

"He's pissed that he wasn't invited to the inauguration of Tegel," Alexej chuckled.

Vladi yearned for another vodka to drown his desperation. The official inauguration ceremony of that damn airport that shouldn't even exist had been two weeks ago. He still couldn't quite believe that the Americans had managed to pull this off.

Building an airport in Moscow would take a year at least, and here this Richards guy had done it in ninety days, with neither heavy machinery nor raw materials readily available. That man must be a veritable magician.

The acting Lord Mayor Louise Schroeder had given a

riveting speech thanking the three Western Kommandanten for their continuous efforts to help the population in Berlin.

Understandably Sokolov wasn't invited, because thanks to the lying media everyone in the West deemed him the beast that was willing to starve an entire city to death for political motives. He'd been in an irascible mood for the past two weeks and apparently urgently needed to find someone to blame for the new airport.

Grigori seemed to read Vladi's thoughts. "If I were you I'd blame it on the black marketeers. Tell him you've been after a ring of smugglers using the Havel river to bring in raw materials for the airport construction and are close to finding the culprit."

"Me? But I don't know anything..." It was the first time he'd heard about this particular ring of smugglers.

"You have twenty minutes to come up with a believable story."

Vladi's drugged mind didn't want to think. In his current state he'd already accepted the inevitable demotion and wished for a job as street sweeper in Moscow. Anything but Siberia.

Somehow he managed to keep upright, with only a slight stagger, when Grigori pushed him into General Sokolov's office.

The general was yelling into the phone, "This is unacceptable! A despicable attack on the sovereignty of the Soviet Union! A cultural outrage! An insult to every citizen in Berlin! A return to fascism!"

The person on the other side of the line seemed to cut him short, because Sokolov grabbed his stomach with a pained grimace and then said in a slightly more civil manner, "Stalin will formally protest against this willful destruction of our property."

Vladi approached the huge meeting table and took the seat furthest from the general. One of his aides was sitting next to Vladi.

"What's happened?" Vladi whispered.

"You haven't heard? Everyone in Berlin must have heard the blast."

Vladi shook his head. Blast? Now that the aide mentioned it, there had been an explosion earlier this day, but Vladi hadn't given it much attention. Probably the detonation of some condemned building. It happened all the time.

"The French hooligans have blasted our radio tower at Tegel."

Vladi was suddenly wide awake. "They did what?"

"Under the excuse that the radio tower is a danger for the air traffic at the new airport they have just blasted it along with the half-finished steel pole that was meant to replace it."

Sokolov had finished insulting whoever was on the other side of the line and turned to address the six men gathered in his office.

"I have just issued my formal protests to General Ganeval. The French Kommandant had the audacity to claim that he can do in his sector whatever he wants and we should just build a new radio tower on our territory."

It was a peculiar situation the Americans, British and French had complained about for the past three years: The Berlin Rundfunk was under Soviet control and didn't give the others a single minute of airtime, but its headquarters was located within the British sector and the transmitter in the French sector. Apparently now they'd found a way to get rid of the radio station broadcasting what they falsely called *hateful Soviet propaganda*.

Vladi saw his chance to get on the good side of Sokolov again. "Comrade General, it is an abhorrent crime against our anti-fascist endeavors, a stab with the dagger in the back of democracy, freedom and brotherhood. We need to avenge this attack on everything that's good and holy."

"What do you suggest?" Sokolov stared directly at Vladi. The general wasn't above personal vengeance and if Vladi could bring him the culprit, or at least a scapegoat for the blasting of the tower, then he'd be able to redeem himself in the general's eyes.

"Comrade General, we know exactly who is to blame for this vicious act and I can present his head to you for punishment."

"Who?"

Vladi actually had no idea, so he mentioned the name of the man whose accomplishment had tortured him for the past two weeks. "Second Lieutenant Victor Richards."

Sokolov seemed to waver. Nobody gave two hoots about abducting one thousand Germans, but harming one American soldier would certainly cause repercussions.

"Discreetly of course," Vladi added.

Ulyanin said, "Comrade General, Comrade Rublev might be on to something. We cannot let this go unpunished, but if the person in question has an accident, nobody can blame us."

But they will still understand the message. Vladi completed Ulyanin's sentence.

General Sokolov gave the slightest nod toward Vladi and then continued with other pressing topics. Vladi's banishment to Siberia had been axed, at least for the time being. Now he just needed to make sure Richards suffered an unfortunate accident.

BRUNI

B runi threw her arms around Victor. "I can't believe you did it. You're my hero. In fact, you're probably the hero of every single West Berliner."

It had been surprisingly easy to convince the French Kommandant that the radio towers needed to be taken down for the security of air traffic. Nobody ever mentioned the welcome side effect that the spewing of hateful propaganda from the Russians would stop at least for a while, but wherever he'd gone with his proposition, Victor had received satisfied nods.

"I love you, you know that. Right?" Bruni said.

"Yes. I know that. I do have to make a confession, though…"

Her eyebrow lifted and worry etched lines into her face.

"Don't worry, it's nothing bad, sweetheart. I was promoted to Second Lieutenant two weeks ago."

"Why didn't you tell me?"

"Because I was afraid you would only love me because I'm an officer now."

She giggled, but then became serious. "You're right. I've always said I need an officer to afford me the lifestyle I want. But then…that was before I fell in love with you. I'd stay with you even if you were a street sweeper."

"Good to know, because I was planning to resign from the Air Force and…" He laughed when he saw the shock in her face. But as soon as she noticed he was just teasing her, she launched at him, tickling him. "You rotten dog, you!"

"It's Sir and Lieutenant, Fräulein!"

"Oh please, Herr Lieutenant, will you forgive my oversight just one more time?" she said, barely able to keep the twinkle of mischief out of her eyes; he had the strongest desire to give her a spanking for being such a bad girl.

"Only if you promise to do everything I want."

The eager light in her eyes became more intense. "I certainly do."

"Always?"

"Always and forever."

"I love you so much."

"I love you, too."

As you can imagine, there will be at least one more book in the series, probably three. The next book changes location from Berlin to Wiesbaden/Frankfurt and is about Zara and the reckless pilot Glenn.

You'll also meet Vladi again and find out whether he

makes good on his promise to involve Victor into a fatal accident.

I don't have a fixed date yet for release, but you can subscribe to my newsletter and will be informed the moment the new book goes on preorder:

http://kummerow.info/subscribe

AUTHOR'S NOTES

Dear Reader,

Thank you so much for reading **On the Brink**. When I began writing the first book in the Berlin Fractured Series **From the Ashes** I had no idea about the incredible amount of research I was about to carry out.

One of my "tasks" was to travel to Berlin and visit the historic locations mentioned in the books, including Karlshorst, the American headquarters and the former airports Tempelhof and Gatow.

Tempelhof is under monument conservation and looks exactly like when it was still in operation, even though the buildings and hangars are now used for different purposes, mostly offices for startup companies. As part of a tour, I visited the airfield, a hangar, and the former administration building – including an indoors basketball hall in the fifth floor – used by the American owners.

The British airport Gatow has been converted into the

Military History Museum and I spent several hours in the exhibitions about everything military aviation from World War I to current times. For aviation enthusiasts I recommend a visit, just for the close to hundred aircraft lined up outside on the field.

One part of the indoors exhibition is dedicated to the Berlin Blockade and Airlift. Together with my visit to the Alliiertenmuseum (Allied Museum) in the former American Headquarters I got a quite detailed idea about the Berlin Blockade and the Airlift.

One of the highlights in the Allied Museum is the Hastings TG 503, a British transport plane from the Airlift era and a French military train, both of which can be visited as part of a tour. There, I had the idea for the scene in which Vladi boards the train and harasses Mrs. Harris.

What was missing to get the complete picture, was the view of the Soviet side. From a friend who grew up in the GDR I knew that the blockade had been explained to them as a "measure of currency controls" that was necessary because of the Western currency reform.

Therefore, I was quite excited to visit the German-Russian Museum in Karlshorst that was called Capitulation Museum until the German re-unification in 1989. There, I found a treasure trove of information about the historical locations, the Soviet Kommandant's office, the signed capitulation, etc. Fictional character Sokolov's office and the stateroom where some of the meetings are held, are described exactly as I found them in the museum.

But there was nothing about the Blockade; it was as if this period had never existed. Instead, there were plenty exhibitions about World War Two and the Soviets' heroic actions, and about the wonderful friendship between East Germany and the Soviet Union. I was utterly disappointed.

My only clue was an excerpt from a newsreel at the Gatow museum, which explained how the Western Allies used the Airlift to steal goods from Berlin and bring them into their zones.

Back home, I searched the internet to hopefully find more of these newsreels, but wasn't successful. What I found instead were some of those awful conspiracy-theory websites along with the deniers who claimed there never was a blockade in the first place. With pseudo-scientific arguments they explain very detailed, how and why this all was a set-up done by the American industrialists who wanted to steal goods from Berlin and sell more airplanes.

Starting from there I found the newspaper *Neues Deutschland*, the former SED party organ that still exists today. As you can imagine it is one of the most left-wing newspapers in existence in Germany and – I bought an archive subscription for it 😱.

They digitalized all their issues starting from the first one in 1945 until the German re-unification in 1989. Most of the chapters written from Vladi's POV are based on newspaper articles. Whenever you think, his or Sokolov's views are exaggerated/ridiculous/impossible, rest assured that I have probably erred on the side of common sense. The Soviets and the communist SED party really propagated this nonsense.

As always, while the historic locations and events are as true to fact as possible, most of the characters are purely fictional, except for General Tunner. I've read his memoir and he will get a much bigger part in the next book in this series, called **In the Skies**. He was not only the brain behind the airlift operations *the Hump* in China and the Berlin Airlift, but also a great supporter of women. He was the first military man to employ women pilots for ferrying operations in the United States during the war.

The demolition of the radio towers at Tegel airport is a true event, but there's no record that it was done to prove undying love to a woman.

Have a wonderful day!

Marion Kummerow

On the Brink (Book 2)

In the Skies (Book 3)

Into the Unknown (Book 4)

Margarete's Story

Turning Point (Prequel)

A Light in the Window

Historical Romance

Second Chance at First Love

Find all my books here:

http://www.kummerow.info

CONTACT ME

I truly appreciate you taking the time to read (and enjoy) my books. And I'd be thrilled to hear from you!
If you'd like to get in touch with me you can do so via

Twitter:
http://twitter.com/MarionKummerow

Facebook:
http://www.facebook.com/AutorinKummerow

Website
http://www.kummerow.info

19048638R00143